# SAVING GRACE

Hannah Howe

Goylake Publishing

Goylake Publishing, Iscoed, 16A Meadow Street, North Cornelly, Bridgend, Glamorgan. CF33 4LL

Print ISBN: 978-0-9933827-9-6
EBook ISBN: 978-1-9996017-2-0

Printed and bound in Britain by Imprint Digital, Exeter, EX5 5HY

Also by Hannah Howe

The Sam Smith Mystery Series
available in print, as eBooks and audio books

*Sam's Song*
*Love and Bullets*
*The Big Chill*
*Ripper*
*The Hermit of Hisarya*
*Secrets and Lies*
*Family Honour*
*Sins of the Father*
*Smoke and Mirrors*
*Stardust*
*Mind Games*
*Digging in the Dirt*
*A Parcel of Rogues*
*Boston*

The Ann's War Mystery Series
available in print, as eBooks and audio books

*Betrayal*
*Invasion*
*Blackmail*
*Escape*
*Victory*

Special thanks to Rebecca Carter, Cusper Lynn and Denise McCabe for their friendship, encouragement and support. And to my readers, without whom...

This book is dedicated to my Victorian ancestors
and, as ever, to my family, with love

# The Western Mail

2 August 1876

## Sensation in the Charles Petrie Case!

Readers may recall that a young banker, by name Mr Charles Petrie, with every opportunity of succeeding in his profession, and commanding a not illiberal income, returned home after riding his horse to dine with his wife, Grace, and her companion, Mrs Quinn. During and after dinner he had nothing to excite him save the receipt of a letter which somewhat annoyed him, and that his wife consumed rather more wine than he considered to be good for her health. Immediately after retiring to his room he was seized with symptoms of irritant poisoning, and despite every effort made on his behalf, he succumbed to its effects. An inquest was held, which vexed the minds of the Coroner's jury to a degree without precedent in Coroners' Inquest Law, and an open verdict was returned. However, the matter will not rest there, for after questions in Parliament, a second inquest has been called under suspicion that Mr Charles Petrie was murdered.

Byronic in his appearance and bohemian in his dress, Daniel Morgan was the antithesis of the successful Victorian advocate, yet successful Victorian advocate he was, at the peak of his powers. However, modesty forbade any form of display or boasting.

Daniel rented an office in Tiger Bay, overlooking the industrial sprawl of Cardiff Docks. The office block, three storeys tall, stood foursquare and proud, a fine example of Victorian architecture.

Rising from his desk, Daniel stood at his second floor office window and stared across the courtyard, to the docks. There, through a shimmering heat haze, he spied the tall masts of the colliers and the coal cutters, ships that transported coal to the four corners of the world. Indeed, thanks to the Valleys and their rich seams of coal, Cardiff was the premier coal port in the world.

In the courtyard, amidst the horses and the carts, the trees and the sniffing dogs, the gentlemen and the fine ladies, Daniel noticed an attractive young woman. In her early twenties, she possessed long, wavy auburn hair, dark brown, serious eyes, a pretty face and a petite form. She wore a red skirt of slender lines complete with a fashionably long bodice and an elegant cascading train. Her clothing clearly defined her natural figure and revealed that she had eschewed the vogue of wearing bulky underwear. To ward off the gentle breezes she had donned a dolman – a short half-mantle with loose sleeves, silk embroidery and a braiding of Chantilly lace. Furthermore, a small hat in white chiffon, trimmed with large red roses, sat well back on her head. The young woman looked around, her gaze uncertain. Then, with the fog clearing from her mind, she entered the building.

With a sigh, Daniel returned to his desk. He glanced across the room, to his assistant, Mr Robeson. At thirty-three, and two years older than Daniel, Mr Robeson possessed dark, lively eyes, a handsome, regal face, smooth ebony skin and a fine goatee beard. However, his bald head and powerful, muscular frame set him apart.

Mr Robeson was studying a local newspaper, reading a report on a recent case, which featured a habitual criminal. On this occasion, Daniel had persuaded the jury to offer leniency. However, Mr Robeson feared that the criminal's nefarious activities would eventually lead him to the gallows.

Before Daniel or Mr Robeson could comment on the newspaper report, a light tapping drew their attention to their office door.

Daniel glanced up from his desk. He tidied his legal papers then said, "Enter."

"Mr Daniel Morgan?" Bathed in the gentle scent of White Rose by Piésse et Lubin, the young woman from the courtyard entered Daniel's office and walked towards his desk.

Immediately, Daniel stood. He nodded. "At your service, ma'am."

"My name is Carys Beaumond, of Beaumond Hall."

"Pleased to make your acquaintance," Daniel said. He waved towards his client's chair, a plush armchair; if you made your clients comfortable, Daniel reasoned, they were tempted to stay and offer you further business. "Please, be seated." He nodded towards his associate. "This is Mr Robeson, my assistant."

"A pleasure to meet you, sir," Carys said, bowing towards Mr Robeson.

In response, the muscular man offered a gentle inclination of his head and an effervescent smile. "Likewise, I am sure."

Daniel waited until Carys had made herself comfortable on his client's chair. Then he returned to his seat. He noted that she had paid no heed to Mr Robeson's ebony skin; some people took offence, while others stared in awe. Her acceptance, plus her pleasing countenance and attractive looks made him smile.

"How may we assist you?" Daniel asked.

"I read about you," Carys said, "in the newspaper, *The Western Mail*. You saved a mother accused of killing her newborn baby. Even though there was no firm evidence in your favour, you convinced the jury at the inquest that the baby was stillborn."

"I believe that to be the truth," Daniel said. "The mother was distraught; she did not murder the child. She buried him out of fear, out of dread that no one would believe her story."

"However," Carys said, "you believed her. And for that reason, I wish to hire you to convince an inquest jury that my friend, Grace Petrie, is innocent of murder."

Daniel frowned. He reached across his desk for a quill pen. "Grace Petrie has been charged with murder?"

"Not as such," Carys said. "However, I fear that the inquest will result in a charge of murder."

"How so?"

From her sleeve, Carys produced a fan. Then, with an elegant, feminine gesture, she waved it in front of her face. Suitably cooled, she said, "Grace's husband of four months, Charles Petrie, was recently poisoned. He swallowed the poison on the 18th April, Easter Tuesday, and endured great agony for three days. Then, sadly, he succumbed to the poison. Initially, Grace suspected suicide. However, the first inquest returned an open verdict. Through Charles' mother, Mary, a second inquest was called. Mary hates Grace – she objected to the marriage and interfered at every opportunity – and through her odium she is determined to lay a charge of murder at Grace's door."

Daniel made a note in his ledger. He wrote in a confident, stylish hand. Looking up, he asked, "Is there any firm reason for the shadow of suspicion to fall upon Grace?"

"There is," Carys said. "You see, Grace was married before, to Captain Gustav Trelawney. Gustav drank alcohol to excess and when drunk he beat Grace. She left him and sued for divorce. This caused a scandal. Her family insisted that she should return to Gustav, and when she refused, they ostracized her."

"And her place in society?" Daniel asked.

"Grace was deemed *persona non grata*. Four years ago, to cure her loneliness, she hired a lady's companion, a Mrs Jennet Quinn. Then, before the divorce papers were served, Gustav died. He had moved to London and was living there with a mistress. He died of alcohol poisoning, which came as no surprise. Indeed, the coroner in London confirmed that as a fact. However, Gustav had not altered his will; probably, at that stage, he was of feeble mind and unable to do so. Therefore Grace, already a wealthy woman, inherited a vast sum of money."

Daniel made another note in his ledger. He paused to consider the note then asked, "May I enquire as to the sum of money?"

"Forty thousand pounds," Carys said.

Daniel glanced at Mr Robeson. Both men widened their eyes. "That is a pretty sum," Daniel said.

"A pretty sum indeed," Carys agreed. "However, then the gossipmongers started to spin their evil tales. Some people had the temerity to suggest that Grace had poisoned Gustav; such words are beyond comprehension for they were living 250 miles apart."

Daniel sat back in his chair. He placed his quill pen in an inkwell. Small bottles of Indian ink lined his desk, their colours bright, vibrant in the sunlight. He stared at the ink then at his potential client, Carys Beaumond. Directly, he asked, "Do you believe in Grace's innocence?"

"I do," Carys said.

"Do you believe that she had no hand in Gustav's passing?"

"I did not know Grace at the time," Carys said. "However, the coroner confirmed that Gustav drank himself to death."

Daniel inclined his head. He examined his

notes then said, "Do you believe that Grace had no hand in Charles' demise?"

"Grace was a loving wife to Charles; I witnessed that with my own eyes."

"How long have you known Grace?" Daniel asked.

"For the past two years."

"That is not a long time."

Carys blushed. She turned her shoulder and applied her fan. With her head held high, she said, "I believe that I am a good judge of character."

"I am sure that you are," Daniel smiled. "However, beyond the past two years you are reliant on Grace's version of events."

"Grace is a truthful person," Carys said, her tone earnest, her features intense; "she would not lie."

"Tell me more about Grace," Daniel said.

Carys paused. She folded her fan. Was this man toying with her? No, he was seeking the truth. While in his office, she would suppress her sensitive nature and place her trust in him.

Turning to face Daniel, Carys said, "After Gustav's death, Grace had everything she could ask for, except her family's love, a husband and her place in society. Then she met Charles Petrie whilst out walking. She swooned to his charm and they married after a brief romance."

"How long was their courtship?"

"Two months," Carys said.

"And how long did the marriage last?"

"Four months," Carys said, "with the addition of two weeks."

"What poison claimed Charles' life?"

"Antimony," Carys said.

Daniel glanced at Mr Robeson, who sat with his features impassive, with his body immobile. Mr Robeson had the ability to absorb great detail and to store that detail in his mind. Although not schooled at university, he was a man of great intellect, an intellect born of experience and a harsh life.

"Antimony is a rare poison," Daniel said.

"So I believe." Carys sat forward. She inclined her head. "Will you accept the brief and act as Grace's advocate?"

"There is the matter of my fee," Daniel said.

"I am a woman of means," Carys smiled; "I will furnish your fee."

Daniel frowned. He liked Carys Beaumond. Indeed, he admired her loyalty to Grace. He felt sure that she was telling the truth. That said, the gaps in Grace's history disturbed him. Daniel had spent a decade talking with fraudsters, with cheats and liars; the woman sitting opposite him was too innocent, too earnest to be counted amongst the likes of them.

To Carys, he said, "The money will come from your account, and not from Grace's purse?"

Carys inclined her head. She said, "Grace feels that she does not require an advocate; in that, she is deluded."

"You must regard Grace as a good friend."

"I do," Carys said.

"Even though she is not welcome in polite society?"

"Grace has done nothing wrong," Carys insisted. "She walked away from a man who abused her. Is that so terrible? Should society shun her because Captain Gustav Trelawney could not hold his drink and later died?"

Daniel sympathised with Carys' argument. However, he decided to play devil's advocate. With a smile, he said, "Some might argue that a woman owes obedience to her father, and then to her husband."

"A woman owes obedience to a man," Carys said, "as long as that man offers her the respect she deserves."

Daniel nodded. Yes, Carys Beaumond was a woman of fine sensibilities. However, she also possessed spirit; she would make a good ally.

After examining his notes, Daniel said, "This brief presents a challenge."

"Are you afraid of a challenge?" Carys

frowned.

"I am not," Daniel said.

"Then what say, you cease your prevaricating and offer me an answer; yea, or nay?"

Daniel stood. He gazed through his office window, to the tall ships floating in the harbour, to the seagulls circling overhead, to the people milling around. The sun was high in the sky, approaching noon. He glanced at the railway tracks, which shimmered in the sunlight. Then he asked Carys, "Did you arrive by train?"

"Yes," she said. "From Pyle Station. I shall meet my maid, Christiana, at Cardiff Station and we shall return by train. Christiana has travelled into town, on my instruction, to purchase lace and sheet music."

"Do you have a love of music?" Daniel asked.

"I play the pianoforte," Carys said.

Daniel smiled at that image. Moreover, he thought, I am willing to wager that you play beautifully. However, returning to the matter in hand, he asked, "Where does Grace live?"

"At Sker, twenty-five miles west of Cardiff, in a manor house called the Grange, two miles west of Beaumond Hall."

Daniel nodded. He studied his diary and noted that the day and forthcoming week contained no items of great import; he could be done with them within an afternoon.

Looking up, he said, "You will permit us the day to study the law journals regarding the inquest into the death of Captain Gustav Trelawney and the first inquest into the death of Charles Petrie."

"But of course," Carys said.

"Excellent," Daniel smiled. "Then we shall meet again, from the first train at Pyle Station tomorrow."

\* \* \*

With the windows open, and with a briny scent in the air, Daniel studied his law journals. Within his journals, he discovered one reference to Captain Gustav Trelawney and the inquest into his death. The jury had returned a verdict of death by misadventure, based upon the post mortem evidence, which confirmed excessive kidney and liver damage, exacerbated by the misuse of alcohol. Heart failure had followed. The coroner had called only a handful of witnesses to this London-based inquest. Nevertheless, Daniel found nothing within the report to challenge the jury's verdict.

The first inquest into the death of Charles Petrie, held locally and more recently, produced two references. Both references were critical of the coroner, Sir Wyndham Trahearne. Daniel knew Sir Wyndham by reputation and through experience;

he judged him a fair and decent man. However, the first inquest had called few witnesses. Moreover, Sir Wyndham had held that inquest at the Grange with tea and biscuits supplied by the staff. The home venue, although not unusual, invited accusations of bias, while Grace Petrie's absence from both inquests, in retrospect, damaged her case.

Daniel concluded that Sir Wyndham had acted in good faith, although with unseemly haste. Under his direction, the inquest had followed a narrow track, which should have led to a verdict of suicide. However, unhappy with the proceedings, the jury had rebelled and returned an open verdict.

Sir Wyndham was the county coroner and therefore duty bound to preside over the second inquest. Nevertheless, the first jury had undermined his authority and Daniel wondered if the coroner had lost a semblance of respect; a ruthless advocate could exploit that vulnerability and turn the inquest into an inquisition, a thought that troubled Daniel as he reached for his supper.

The following day, Daniel and Mr Robeson travelled west on the Great Western Railway. A quarter of a century old, the railway had transformed the towns, the coastal plain and the valleys, transporting iron, coal and limestone. People too had climbed aboard, seeking the seaside for pleasure. All this commerce meant work, and wealth, for the lawyers, as they drew up contracts and administered land deals. However, Daniel considered such work as dry in the extreme, money for money's sake; he preferred the cut and thrust of criminal cases; a fencer by inclination, he relished the challenge; a competitor by nature, he sided with the underdog.

With the morning sun warming the backs of their necks, Daniel and Mr Robeson alighted at Pyle Railway Station. There, they met Carys Beaumond, who was standing beside a matt-black landau, twirling a pink parasol above her head.

"Where is your driver?" Daniel asked.

"Today," Carys smiled. "I shall drive." Lifting her skirt, she climbed aboard the landau, her movements displaying her customary grace. Comfortably seated, she glanced at Daniel. Then, with a dexterous manoeuvre, she took hold of the reins. "It is fun to drive," she said, "don't you think?"

Daniel glanced at Mr Robeson. Meanwhile, Mr Robeson admired the landau's two stalwart horses and merely smiled.

With skill and ease, Carys guided the landau through the villages of Pyle and Corneli, passing Beaumond Hall along the way. The villages were neat and clean. Indeed, their houses displayed white doorsteps despite the fact that many belonged to colliers who garnered coal from the local coalmines.

The metalled road gave way to a dirt track as Carys approached a vast swathe of sand dunes. There, amongst the sand dunes, Daniel spied an imposing manor house, known locally as the Grange.

Isolated and framed by the Severn Sea, the Grange shimmered like an oasis within the sand dunes. Its walls were tall and covered in ivy, while the numerous windows were criss-crossed and patterned with lead. Originally, a medieval grange founded by the Cistercians, the building had developed over the centuries into a manor house.

Carys eased the landau into the courtyard. There, Daniel and Mr Robeson dismounted and placed their feet on the shale. While Mr Robeson gathered their bags, which contained numerous law books, legal documents and a change of clothing,

Daniel offered Carys his right hand. Suitably supported, she joined her companions on the shale. Then, with a twirl of her parasol, she walked across the courtyard towards the main door.

A footman opened the door. A tall, middle-aged man burdened with large ears and a lugubrious expression, in dutiful tones he announced the guests.

Carys thanked the footman. Then, accompanied by Daniel and Mr Robeson, she walked into the morning room where she met Grace. While the women greeted each other, Daniel took stock of his client.

In her early thirties and of small build, Grace possessed soft feminine features, large violet-blue eyes and a clear complexion. Her hair, chestnut in colour, was styled in ringlets and highlighted with blonde streaks. To Daniel, her appearance brought to mind the paintings of Jean-Baptiste Greuze, in particular the sensual nature of the woman in *The White Hat* and the fragile beauty of the girl in *The Broken Vessel*.

Turning to face Daniel, Carys made the introductions. "Grace, this is Mr Daniel Morgan, the famous advocate, and this is his assistant, Mr Robeson."

Daniel bowed towards Grace. He said, "My name has appeared in the newspapers, in connection with a handful of cases; I contend that such coverage does not amount to fame."

"You are famous," Carys insisted. She waved her parasol to indicate that she would brook no argument. Then, she turned towards Grace. "I contend that Mr Morgan should speak for you at the inquest; I will meet the expense."

"Thank you, Carys," Grace said; "your guests are welcome; however, I do not require an advocate."

With an air of indifference, Grace walked into the corridor and then into her drawing room. At Carys' insistence, Daniel and Mr Robeson offered their presence.

Within the drawing room, Daniel admired a suite of rich blue satin, the matching wall hangings, the woollen rugs and an ebonized cabinet inlaid with ivory. China ornaments, carrying the Dresden stamp, decorated the cabinet, while two marble busts of Grecian style looked on.

Grace walked past her embroidery and a novel by George Elliot, which sat on a nest of tables. Then she pulled a silken sash to summon her maid. "Would you care for a glass of sherry, Mr Morgan?" she asked.

Before Daniel could reply, two Skye terriers bounded into the drawing room and ran towards Grace. Immediately, she squatted and kissed them.

While the dogs rewarded their mistress with affection, Daniel said, "Yes, thank you, ma'am; a glass of sherry would be most welcome."

"And what about you, Mr Robeson?" Grace enquired.

"That would be a pleasure, ma'am," Mr Robeson said.

A maid entered, carrying a silver tray laden with a decanter and four thimble-sized glasses. She placed the tray on a table of Spanish mahogany, which occupied a central place within the drawing room. The maid poured sherry from the decanter into each glass. Then she handed a glass to Carys, Grace, Daniel and Mr Robeson, in turn. The maid was young, Daniel noted, barely twenty-one years of age. She possessed a slender figure, a pretty face and an impish smile.

"Thank you, Florrie," Grace said to the maid. "Please, take the dogs with you."

Florrie straightened her white apron. She inclined her head, in dutiful fashion. Then she called the dogs, Meg and Mrs Dot, and reached for the tray.

"Leave the tray and decanter," Grace insisted. "I am sure that our guests must be thirsty; after all, it is a very warm day."

Florrie the maid left the drawing room with the Skye terriers at her heels. At ease, Daniel, Carys and

Mr Robeson sipped their sherry while Grace consumed her drink in one gulp, which was not a good sign, Daniel reasoned.

"This is a beautiful decanter," Daniel said, addressing a fine glass vessel, placed with pride atop the ebonized cabinet. He sniffed the vessel. "It smells faintly of Marsala."

"Thank you," Grace smiled. "I acquired that decanter in Italy, in Venice, whilst on holiday. I kept it by my bedside, to supply my regular nightcap of Marsala. Unfortunately, during a restless night, I disturbed the decanter and it fell on to the floor. The glass fractured. I disposed of the Marsala. However, for fear that the glass might shatter, I did not wash the decanter." She sighed in wistful fashion, as though recalling a distant memory. "The decanter invokes special memories; therefore, I decided to keep it as an ornament."

Daniel nodded. He sipped his sherry. Meanwhile, Grace replenished her glass.

After Grace had consumed her second glass of sherry, she turned to Mr Robeson and said, "Sir, you are not a native of these parts."

"I am from Nevis," Mr Robeson replied, "in the West Indies."

"And how did you arrive here?" Grace asked.

"I took to the seas as a sailor. The currents brought me to Tiger Bay."

"Where you found Mr Morgan?"

Mr Robeson toasted his friend and colleague. With a bow, he offered an effervescent smile. "Indeed," he said.

Daniel placed his empty glass on the tray. Then he straightened, with a mind for business. "The first inquest into the death of Charles Petrie dismissed the notion of suicide; the jury concluded that your husband did not kill himself. Therefore, it seems likely that the second inquest will push for a verdict of murder."

"Charles' mother will push for that verdict," Grace said, her tone bitter, laced with acid, "to save her son's good name. However, I did not kill my husband."

"Who murdered Charles?"

"I do not know," Grace said. She shook her head in sorrowful fashion. Then, once again, she reached for the sherry.

While Grace poured sherry from the decanter into her glass, Daniel walked over to a mahogany sideboard. There, he studied a photograph, set in a silver frame. The camera had captured its subject, a man in his early thirties, in the midst of an unfortunate moment, with his eyes half-closed. The man possessed dark hair, parted on the right, heavy-lidded eyes, large side-whiskers, a proud nose and a sullen mouth. The image did not flatter him. Indeed, he looked cold and somewhat aloof.

"Is this your late husband?" Daniel asked.

"It is," Grace replied.

"Could you please tell me something about him?"

"What would you like to know?" Grace frowned.

"His profession..."

"Charles was a banker. He harboured an ambition to enter parliament."

Daniel glanced at the photograph. Yes, he thought, such a profession would have suited him well.

However, he said to Grace, "If I am to speak for you, I am afraid that I must pry into your private life."

Grace stood. She walked to the window. There, she stared sightlessly through the leaded glass. "This is a charade," she cried; "I did not kill my husband; I do not require an advocate."

Carys stood too, rising from her satin chair. "If you would prefer," she said, "I shall leave the room while you talk with Mr Morgan."

With a sigh, Grace turned and walked over to her friend. She took hold of Carys' hands and held them in affectionate fashion. "I hold no secrets from you," she said. "I hold no secrets from anyone; pray, please stay."

Carys inclined her head. Then she resumed her seat on the fine satin chair.

"Mr Morgan," Grace said, "do you really believe that the second inquest will seek to prove murder?"

"The first inquest returned an open verdict, casting doubt on the notion of suicide. Therefore, if not to establish murder, why hold a second inquest?"

Ashen-faced, Grace slumped on to her seat of blue satin. Once again, she reached for the decanter, spilling a considerable measure of sherry on to the silver tray. With an unsteady hand, she raised the glass to her lips. She drank the sherry, her face revealing a dark grimace. Then she asked, "What would you like to know, Mr Morgan?"

"In my experience," Daniel said, "murder is committed for one of three main reasons – as an act of violent barbarism, as an act of passion, or as an act of financial gain; you live in a beautiful house; therefore, I assume that your needs do not stretch to financial gain."

"I inherited £40,000 from Gustav, my first husband. I brought £20,000 into that marriage. I would not marry, and certainly I would not murder, for financial gain."

"And what of Charles," Daniel asked, "what did he bring into your second marriage?"

"One hundred pounds," Grace said.

Daniel raised an eyebrow, an act mimicked by Mr Robeson, who stood by the fireplace. "One hundred pounds," Daniel said, "compared with £40,000 does not sound like a fair match."

"Charles was limited to a small allowance bestowed upon him by his mother; she controlled him through her finances."

"However," Daniel said, "surely his profession as a banker brought its own rewards."

"Charles liked to speculate on stocks and shares," Grace said; "he was a poor speculator. Plus, he owed £500 to an erstwhile mistress."

"He maintained a mistress?"

"Yes," Grace said. "And she bore him a child. He financed their upkeep."

"He told you of this before your marriage?"

"He did."

"And you told him of your first husband, and the scandal of suing for divorce?"

"I did."

"When you married Charles," Daniel asked, "did that union of your hearts produce a union of your finances?"

"It did not."

Daniel inclined his head. He smiled quietly to himself. "You invoked the Married Woman's Property Act?"

"I did."

"Despite the marriage, you secured your finances and possessions in your own name; that must have annoyed your husband."

"It did," Grace confessed. "Charles was furious with me. It led to many bitter arguments."

"Did the servants overhear those arguments?" Daniel asked.

"Possibly," Grace said; "you will have to ask them."

"Upon Charles' death," Daniel said, "how much did you inherit?"

"One hundred pounds."

"And upon your death, what would Charles have inherited?"

"I made a will on my honeymoon," Grace said; "I left everything to him."

Daniel mulled over the facts, as presented by Grace. He saw no reason to doubt her word. However, the huge financial imbalance, the vast fiscal gulf between Charles and Grace, disturbed him.

"You mentioned arguments," Daniel said.

"Over money. And we argued when his mother interfered in our marriage; at other times, we were happy. At least," Grace sighed, "I thought we were happy."

Daniel glanced at the photograph of the man

with the hooded eyes. When open, did those eyes sparkle with vitality, or did those heavy lids bear a darker burden? Despite the verdict delivered by the first jury, did Charles Petrie commit suicide?

Turning to Grace, Daniel asked, "Did Charles endure periods of melancholy?"

"He threatened to leave the marriage."

"On one occasion?"

"On several occasions," Grace said.

"Yet," Daniel reasoned, "you were only married for a touch over four months."

"Nevertheless," Grace said, "he suggested that we should separate, and divide the money equally between us."

Daniel glanced at Mr Robeson. A man of the world, Mr Robeson merely shook his head and shrugged.

"It pains me to say this," Daniel said to Grace Petrie; "however, have you considered that Charles married you, not for love, but for your money?"

"Sadly," Grace said, "I have reached that conclusion."

"And if an advocate should suggest to a jury that you murdered your husband to regain your freedom and secure your fortune?"

"Surely," Grace frowned, "they would not believe him."

"Juries can be fickle," Daniel said; "often, they

will latch on to a fact, an insignificant detail, and that will colour a case."

Grace stood. She walked over to the chimney breast. There, she pulled a silken sash to summon her maid. When Florrie appeared, Grace said, "I believe that we require another decanter of sherry."

* * *

Grace consumed three more glasses of sherry. Then she felt in need of fresh air.

While Carys offered Mr Robeson a tour of the local landscape, Daniel walked with Grace around her beautifully maintained gardens. Daniel noted that in spite of the sandy soil trees, roses and wisteria all prospered, especially the roses, which Grace had massed together in huge beds. He also spied ducks, geese and fantail pigeons, wildlife that roamed through the orchards, strutted across the lawns, and perched on the various nooks and crannies, offered by the Grange.

"You have beautiful gardens," Daniel said.

"Flowers are my hobby," Grace smiled. She walked on. Then she faltered, placing a hand to her forehead. "May we rest," she pleaded, "I feel faint."

Daniel took hold of Grace's left elbow; he led her to a bench, which looked out, across the yellow and green of the sand dunes to the blue waters of the Severn Sea.

When Grace had positioned herself comfortably upon the bench, Daniel asked, "Do you often feel faint?"

"On occasion," Grace said. "Also, my back troubles me and, at times, I feel nauseous."

"Have you consulted a doctor?" Daniel frowned.

Grace inclined her head. She said, "I should tell you now, Mr Morgan, that on the 6th April, I suffered a miscarriage, my second miscarriage in three months."

"And your doctor attributes your poor health to your miscarriages?"

"He does."

Daniel paused to admire the scenery. Far out to sea, he spied ships, vessels that might have sailed from Tiger Bay, from the harbour outside his office window. While, closer to the shore, seagulls squawked and hovered, as they searched for luncheon, as they scavenged for a meal that would tide them through the day.

Grace closed her eyes. She allowed the sun to kiss her face. The sun also warmed her bosom, through the low, square cut of her dress. That dress would draw many admiring glances, Daniel reckoned. However, it would not sit well with the jury or the coroner.

As Grace opened her eyes, Daniel said, "I believe that you and Gustav were married for seven years."

"We were," Grace said.

"May I ask, did you miscarry during that marriage?"

"I did not."

"Yet, that marriage was not blessed with any children."

Grace tilted her head to her left. She frowned, as though perplexed. "You ask the strangest questions, Mr Morgan, and you make the strangest observations."

"Sometimes," Daniel smiled, "my questions and observations bear no fruit, other times they lead to a harvest."

"In reply to your observation," Grace said, "my first marriage was not blessed with any children."

"Could you offer a reason for that?"

Grace averted her gaze. She stared at the ground. "Gustav kept a mistress," she said, her voice fragile, revealing her pain; "he was drawn to other women."

"And when you were with him," Daniel asked, "was he drawn to you?"

"On occasion," Grace said. "Often, he was drunk; at those times, he took his pleasure through venting his spleen."

"He hit you."

Grace looked up. She met Daniel's gaze. "Repeatedly," she said.

"Did he ever try to explain his behaviour?"

"No. I assumed that he hit me because of the wine."

"Why did Gustav drink to excess?"

"I cannot think of a reason," Grace said.

"He was a captain; he served as a soldier."

"In the cavalry," Grace explained.

"Did his experiences in battle unnerve him?"

"He served in the cavalry; however, he did not participate in any major battles," Grace said.

"Therefore," Daniel mused, "we can only speculate on his over-fondness for wine."

"Sadly, that is true," Grace agreed.

"Did Charles drink to excess?"

"He drank burgundy, and brandy, in moderation."

"You have a taste for sherry," Daniel said.

Grace inclined her head. Then, with the colour rising on her cheeks, she turned away. In a small voice, she said, "Charles believed that I drank beyond common reason."

"What happened on the night Charles was taken ill?"

Grace stood. Regaining the strength in her legs, she walked away. "Must I discuss this again?" she complained.

"If I am to be of any assistance," Daniel said, "I am afraid you must."

Grace walked into the orchard, into the shade. At a leisurely pace, Daniel followed. The sun was high in the noonday sky, warming the apples on the trees. Grace reached up, to touch an apple. Then she pulled away as though it were the forbidden fruit.

While gazing wistfully into the distance, she said, "That fateful night we had dinner."

"What did you eat?"

"A meal of whiting, roast lamb, eggs and anchovies. Charles was in bad humour, so he refused the fish course."

"What did you drink?"

Grace sighed. Once again, she stared down to the dry ground. "Mrs Quinn, my lady's companion, and I drank two bottles of sherry, while Charles consumed his usual four glasses of burgundy."

"And what of your actions after the meal?"

"After the meal, we retired to our rooms. At that time, we were sleeping in separate rooms, on account of my second miscarriage. Mrs Quinn slept in the bedroom with me, to tend to my needs. That day was my first day out after my confinement. By train, I travelled to Cardiff, with Mrs Quinn, and by evening, I felt exhausted. Upon our return, Charles offered us a warm greeting. Then he went riding and his horse bolted. That placed him in a foul mood. Furthermore, he was suffering from a toothache, had lost money on the stock market and had received an angry letter from his mother. In my bedroom, Mrs Quinn brushed out my hair. Then I put on my nightgown, drank a glass of Marsala, and went to bed. I fell asleep in seconds. I am not sure how long I slept. At one point, I heard Florrie calling me. She said Charles was ill and I should come quickly. Naturally, I rushed out of bed."

"Did you place your dressing gown around your shoulders?" Daniel asked.

"No, I did not. But later, when the doctors arrived, and when I felt a chill, I did." Grace shivered, as though recalling the moment in vivid detail. Then she placed a hand against a tree, for support. "I found Charles in his bedroom. He looked very pale, very ill. I asked him what troubled him so. However, before he could reply, he vomited; Mrs Quinn and Florrie tended him and under Mrs Quinn's instruction, Florrie disposed of the vomit and cleaned the bowl. I ran down the hall, screaming at the servants to summon a doctor. Pegram, our groom, saddled a horse and rode at speed to Dr Marsh's house."

"Mrs Quinn reached Charles before you did?"

"Yes," Grace said. "She was sitting at my bedside, fully dressed. Florrie summoned her first, then she called me."

"Did Mrs Quinn summon a doctor?"

"Yes, she did," Grace said. "She summoned Dr Spofforth. However, Dr Marsh lived nearer, so I summoned him."

"Why did Mrs Quinn summon Dr Spofforth when Dr Marsh lived nearer?" Daniel asked. He scratched his forehead, genuinely perplexed.

"I do not know the answer to your question," Grace said. "Both doctors arrived and, over the three days that Charles lay stricken, I summoned four more doctors, but none could save him."

"Did any of the doctors suspect poison?" Daniel asked.

"May we return to the Grange?" Grace frowned. "I find the heat stifling; I should have brought my fan."

Daniel inclined his head. He offered Grace his right arm. Then he escorted her to a bench, which sat under the drawing room window. This window looked out across the sand dunes, to mounds of green and gold that extended for as far as the eye could see.

Grace sat on the bench while Daniel remained standing. He prompted, "Did any of the doctors in attendance suspect poison?"

"Not at first," Grace said. "They believed that Charles had taken too much laudanum, for his toothache."

"Was he in the habit of taking laudanum?"

"Yes," Grace said, "for his teeth and gums. Professor Pennington, who arrived on the second day, he suspected poison. Later, through an autopsy, he confirmed the presence of antimony in Charles' body."

"Was Charles lucid during his suffering?" Daniel asked.

"He was, for most of the time."

"Did he blame anyone for his suffering?"

"No, he did not. He was kindness itself to me, to Mrs Quinn and all the servants."

"I would like to talk with the servants," Daniel said, "and explore the rooms within your house."

"You are free to do so," Grace bowed.

Daniel glanced to his left. There, he spied Mr Robeson, who was walking towards the Grange. To Daniel's regret, he caught no sight of Carys Beaumond; presumably, she had returned to the Hall.

"Your fee, Mr Morgan," Grace said, "that will come from my purse."

"The source of my fee is between you and Carys Beaumond," Daniel smiled.

"Now," Grace sighed, placing a weary hand to her forehead, "I must rest and quench my thirst; my throat is very dry after our prolonged conversation."

Daniel escorted Grace into her drawing room. Then he stepped into the courtyard to greet Mr Robeson.

"We must secure lodgings," Daniel said. "The train, to and from Cardiff each day, would consume too much time."

"I have already done so," Mr Robeson grinned. "Through Carys Beaumond's recommendation, I have secured rooms, in the inn, yonder. The rooms are comfortable and they offer a view of the Grange."

Daniel followed Mr Robeson's gaze to an isolated building, which sat inland. The building was fifty to sixty years old, Daniel estimated. Smaller than the Grange, it would offer a measure of home comforts.

"Talk with the servants," Daniel said; "discover what they remember about the night Charles was taken ill. I will examine his bedroom and talk with Florrie, the maid."

* * *

With Grace's permission, Daniel wandered around the Grange. He found the cellar well stocked with wine, brandy, burgundy, champagne and Marsala. Climbing the cellar steps to the ground floor, he discovered a kitchen, conservatory, butler's pantry, morning room, dining room, drawing room, library and a room that appeared to serve no distinct purpose. All the rooms were well maintained while Grace had decorated the family rooms with fine glass and crystal. However, Daniel's eyes alighted on the exquisitely crafted furniture. His father was a cabinetmaker; a skilled artisan, he received a modest reward for his considerable ability. Nevertheless, Daniel's father had scrimped and saved to send him to the finest schools, buying votes when necessary to secure his selection.

The second floor contained the servants' quarters. A private storey of the Grange, Daniel decided that he would not venture into those rooms today. Besides, the first floor had captured his attention. On that floor, he discovered two spare bedrooms, a bathroom, Charles' bedroom, Grace's bedroom, plus Charles' dressing room and Grace's wardrobe. Grace's wardrobe was three times the size of Charles' dressing room, he noted with wry amusement.

Daniel paid particular attention to Charles' bedroom, the room where the poor fellow had died. In the bedroom, he noticed a bay window and a smaller side window. The room also contained a grate, a gas lamp, a large bed and a chest of drawers. A small clock sat on top of the drawers, its loud tick intruding upon the silence.

In Charles' bathroom, Daniel discovered a medicine cabinet. However, someone had removed all the medicine bottles. Stains remained. Moreover, those stains revealed that, at one time, Charles had kept the cabinet well stocked.

As Daniel observed the stains, Florrie, the maid, entered Charles' bedroom. He joined her in the bedroom, beside the bay window.

Shuffling her dainty feet, Florrie offered a nervous smile. She bowed towards Daniel. "You wish to see me, sir?"

"Yes, thank you," Daniel said.

In turn, he smiled at the young woman. She wore a white apron, a long black dress and a white cap, trimmed with white lace, clothes that sat neatly upon her slight frame. She had drawn her fair hair into a bun, in businesslike fashion, while her lively blue eyes suggested that they would miss nothing, or at least nothing of great importance.

"Your name is Florrie," Daniel said.

"Florrie Williams, sir," the maid bowed.

"There is no need to bow when you address me," Daniel said, "for I am a servant here too."

"Sorry, sir," Florrie said, catching herself in mid-bow.

"How long have you been in service?" Daniel asked.

"Two years and two months with Mrs Petrie. Before that, I was a parlour maid for Mrs Prior."

"For what length of time?"

"Six years, sir."

"You left school at thirteen?"

"Yes, sir."

"So, you are twenty-one?"

"Yes, sir."

"Why did you leave Mrs Prior?"

"She died, sir; she was quite elderly."

Daniel inclined his head. He gazed through the window, to a maze of hedgerows that stretched towards the orchard. Grace's dogs, Meg and Mrs Dot, were running around the orchard. In turn, they squatted to relieve themselves.

With his eyes on the maid, Daniel asked, "Do you enjoy your work, Florrie?"

"Very much, sir."

"Do you like Mrs Petrie?"

"Very much, sir."

"Did you like Mr Petrie?"

"Very much, sir," Florrie nodded with vigour.

"Away from work, what brings you pleasure?"

"Dancing, sir. And I take satisfaction from singing in the chapel."

"Are your parents alive?" Daniel asked.

"Yes, sir. My father is a collier; my mother keeps house and tends my two younger brothers and two younger sisters."

"Do you have a suitor?" Daniel smiled.

Florrie looked away. As she turned back, she offered the advocate a shy smile. "Not at the moment, sir; all my hours are consumed with my duties."

Daniel paused. Then he invited Florrie into the bathroom. There, he examined the medicine cabinet, paying particular attention to the oblong and circular stains.

"What happened to the bottles in this cabinet?" Daniel asked.

"A policeman removed them, sir."

"Can you recall the nature of the bottles that resided in this cabinet?"

"It was not my business to look, sir."

"However," Daniel smiled, "when the policeman removed the bottles surely out of curiosity or common interest, you allowed yourself a casual peep?"

Florrie glanced over her shoulder, to the medicine cabinet. A hint of mischief sparkled in her bright blue eyes. "Well, sir, it was not my place to look, but I believe that the policeman removed bottles of laudanum, chloroform, Condy's Fluid, a packet of Epsom Salts and a phial of camphor liniment."

Daniel made a mental note of Florrie's list.

Then he asked the observant maid, "Were the police called the night Mr Petrie was taken ill?"

"No, sir; they arrived several weeks later, after the first inquest."

Daniel sighed; in the search for justice, the police would offer little in this case. In reflective mood, he returned to the bedroom.

While staring at Charles' bed, Daniel said, "You discovered Mr Petrie *in extremis*?"

"In what, sir?" Florrie frowned, the faint lines upon her forehead deepening in concentration.

"In great pain," Daniel explained.

"Yes, sir."

Daniel walked around the bed. He paused then said, "Tell me, Florrie, what happened that evening?"

"Well, sir, the mistress and the master retired to their bedrooms, in keeping with their recent custom. I filled the master's pitcher with fresh water, in keeping with my custom. Then the master asked me to run his bath."

"Did he drink from the pitcher?" Daniel asked.

"The master drank from the pitcher every night, sir; that was his custom."

"Did he use a tumbler?"

"No, sir; he always drank from the pitcher."

"After his bath," Daniel asked, "did you throw the bath water away?"

"No, sir; at least, not straight away."

"Why not?"

"Because the master told me to leave it; he said he would use it again in the morning."

Daniel inclined his head. Although not hygienic, retaining bath water overnight was a common, practical custom.

"Therefore," Daniel reasoned, "Mr Petrie's thoughts were on the morning."

"Yes, sir."

"Which means that he was not contemplating suicide."

"The master would never take his own life, sir," Florrie insisted; "he was not of that sort."

"What happened after the bath?" Daniel asked.

"I was making my way downstairs when the master called out, 'Grace! Grace! Hot water! Hot water!'"

"Those were his exact words?"

"Yes, sir."

"He called for hot water to make himself vomit?"

"I believe so, sir."

Daniel paused. He glanced around the bedroom in thoughtful fashion then asked, "Subsequently, what did you do?"

"I knocked on the mistress' door and Mrs Quinn answered."

"They didn't hear the commotion?"

"Apparently not, sir. I told Mrs Quinn that the master was ill and she said that she would tend to him because the mistress was asleep. Then I followed Mrs Quinn into the master's bedroom. He ran towards the window and was sick several times."

"This window?" Daniel asked. He opened the bay window and peered down to the ground.

"Yes, sir; that is correct."

"There are tiles below this window," Daniel observed, "above the drawing room window."

"Yes, sir," Florrie said. "The master was sick on the leads."

"What happened to the vomit?" Daniel asked.

"Professor Pennington told me to collect the vomit in a clean jar with a silver spoon. He arrived on the second day. But it rained overnight and the rain washed some of the vomit away."

"What happened next?" Daniel asked.

"With Mrs Quinn's help, I brought the master to his bed. We removed his nightshirt, cleaned his face, and he was sick again. Then Mrs Quinn ordered me to run downstairs, to mix mustard in a cup of water, and to brew a warm cup of coffee. But first I ran to the mistress' bedroom and roused her because I thought she should know about the master."

"What was Grace's reaction?"

"She was in a deep sleep, so she was confused at first. Then she jumped up and ran to the master's bedroom."

"After rousing Grace, you went downstairs to mix the mustard in water and make a cup of coffee?"

"I did, sir. Then I brought the mustard and the coffee to the master's bedroom, along with a bowl. He was sick into the bowl."

"What happened to the bowl?"

"Mrs Quinn ordered me to clean it. Then Mrs Quinn encouraged the master to drink the coffee, but his teeth were clenched. She managed to force some of the coffee into his mouth, but he was sick again. Then the mistress ran into the corridor screaming for a doctor."

Daniel inclined his head. He said, "I understand that Mrs Quinn had already sent for a doctor."

"I don't know about that, sir; she must have sent for him whilst I was in the kitchen. Anyway, within the hour two doctors arrived."

"At this stage," Daniel asked, "did you suspect poison?"

"No, sir. I thought the master had suffered a fit, because he had been out riding and his horse had bolted."

"Did Mrs Quinn stay with Mr Petrie throughout the evening?"

"Throughout the evening, sir, and well into the night."

"And Mrs Petrie?"

"She stayed with the master too. After the doctors arrived, the mistress became exhausted and she fell asleep beside him. Then Mrs Quinn told me to leave the room."

"Where is Mrs Quinn now?" Daniel asked.

"She left the mistress' service after the first inquest. Now, I believe that she rents a room in Porthcawl, overlooking the seafront."

"Thank you, Florrie," Daniel said.

"My pleasure, sir." Florrie inclined her head. She smiled. "Will that be all?"

Daniel returned her smile. He said, "That will be all, for today."

On Daniel's instruction, Mr Robeson rented a landau. Although the landau was not as fine as Carys Beaumond's vehicle, it served Daniel well on his three-mile journey along the metalled roads and dirt tracks to Porthcawl.

At Porthcawl, Daniel strolled along the seafront. There, he inquired after Mrs Jennet Quinn. He discovered that she rented a room in a guest house near the harbour, in a practical, economical location.

Porthcawl harbour was quiet, with few boats bobbing on the water. Indeed, the docks at Cardiff were sucking the life out of the local harbour. Therefore, the town was in a state of flux. On the one hand, it still served industry through the transportation of coal and limestone, while on the other hand, and with an eye to the future, guest houses and hotels catered for travellers and holidaymakers; the town elders had recognized that, nowadays, people of all classes were seeking the pleasures of a seaside resort.

Daniel climbed the stairs to Mrs Quinn's first floor accommodation. There, he knocked on a badly splintered door and awaited an answer. Eventually, a woman opened the door, just a fraction; she peered through the gap, through small, round, wire-framed spectacles, which sat high on the bridge of her slender nose.

"Mrs Quinn?" Daniel enquired.

"Yes," she said in a small, barely audible voice.

"My name is Daniel Morgan. I am an advocate. I will speak for Grace Petrie at the forthcoming inquest into the death of Charles Petrie. I understand that you were Grace's close companion for over four years; therefore, I would like to speak with you."

Mrs Quinn hesitated. At all times, she maintained a strong grip on the splintered door with her nervous right hand. However, after some thought, she relented and opened the door. "Very well," she said; "you had better come in."

Daniel followed Mrs Quinn into her boxroom. He noted a simple bed, a chest of drawers, a small stove and a wicker chair. The floorboards were bare, devoid of any carpet. Indeed, the room seemed a world away from the luxury she had enjoyed at the Grange.

As for the woman herself, Daniel noted, she wore black clothing, which matched her tightly bound, silver-streaked ebony hair. Her skin, olive in colour, revealed the passing of at least fifty birthdays, while her wrinkles and skin tone suggested many days spent in the sun.

Daniel waited while Mrs Quinn removed her

embroidery from the wicker chair. With great care, she placed the needlework on her bed. Then she sat on the chair, while Daniel remained standing, near the door.

He said, "You are a widow, Mrs Quinn."

In her small voice, she replied, "Does it show in my demeanour?"

"You live alone," Daniel explained; "I see no husband."

"Joshua died many years ago, whilst at work, in Ireland."

"What was Joshua's profession?"

"He was a civil engineer."

Daniel inclined his head in sympathy. Then he asked, "Did your marriage produce any children?"

"Three boys," Mrs Quinn said. "I buried a daughter as an infant."

Once again, Daniel's face displayed his sympathy. "Your boys are not with you," he observed.

"They are away," Mrs Quinn said, "in boarding school."

"That must be expensive," Daniel said.

"I have my savings. And Mrs Petrie rewarded me well, when I served as her companion."

"And what of the future," Daniel asked, "and your financial security?"

"I have relatives in Ireland. There is the

prospect of a small inheritance."

As Mrs Quinn spoke, she drew minute circles upon her skirt with her nervous right hand. Meanwhile, behind her, the sun shone through a small window, highlighting the dust motes, warming the window frame, casting a shadow in the form of an elongated cross.

Daniel stepped out of the shadow. Then he said, "You were Mrs Petrie's companion for over four years."

"That is correct."

"And before that appointment?"

"I was a governess."

"How did you meet Mrs Petrie?" Daniel asked.

"She was staying at her solicitor's house, during a period of separation from her first husband, Captain Gustav Trelawney. I was educating the solicitor's children."

"And Grace asked you to become her companion?"

"Not immediately," Mrs Quinn said. "We talked generally for four or five months before we discussed terms."

"However," Daniel said, "after the first inquest, you parted company with Grace; for any reason?"

Mrs Quinn lowered her head. Her fingers, forever restless, drew frantic circles over the lace in her black skirt. In a whisper, she said, "You must ask Mrs Petrie that question."

"You tended Mr Petrie on the night he was taken ill."

"Yes," Mrs Quinn said, "before the doctors arrived."

"You called for Dr Spofforth and not Dr Marsh, even though Dr Marsh lived nearer."

Mrs Quinn stared at her fingers, which continued to draw small circles upon her skirt. In her customary whisper, she said, "At the time, I thought that Dr Spofforth was better suited to Mr Petrie's condition."

"You immediately suspected poison?"

"No," she said, "initially, I suspected chloroform."

"How so?"

"I smelled it on his breath."

"And later," Daniel asked, "did you suspect poison?"

"Later," Mrs Quinn said, "I knew that Charles had swallowed poison."

"How so?"

"He told me." She looked up, smiled, and spoke the words as a simple fact.

"What did he say?"

"He said, 'I have taken poison; don't tell Grace.'"

"Why, 'don't tell Grace?'"

"Not to upset her, I suppose."

"However," Daniel reasoned, "Grace would have discovered the truth, soon enough."

"Charles was in great distress," Mrs Quinn said; "sometimes, his words did not make sense."

"However, he definitely said, 'I have taken poison?'"

"Those were his words, yes."

"To claim his own life?"

Mrs Quinn inclined her head. She said, "I assumed so."

"However," Daniel said, "the night Charles swallowed the poison, he was thinking of his morning bath."

"I cannot tell you what Charles was thinking," Mrs Quinn said, a tetchy note troubling her voice.

"Also," Daniel said, "people who claim their own lives are looking to escape pain, of the mind or of the body, yet antimony brings on great pain; it is not a suicide drug."

"I would not know," Mrs Quinn said; "I have no great knowledge of medicines."

"Yet, you nursed Grace when she was ill, when she was in recovery from her miscarriages."

Mrs Quinn smiled, though the amusement did not touch her eyes. "I should have said, 'I have a limited knowledge of medicines.'"

Daniel paused to assess the woman and her

words. He noted that she had repeatedly called Charles by his given name, which indicated a familiarity beyond the normal master-servant relationship.

While considering the nature of Charles and Mrs Quinn's relationship, he asked, "What was Charles' mood on the evening of his illness?"

"He was distressed," Mrs Quinn said, "troubled, agitated."

"How so?"

"His horse had bolted and galloped five miles. Also, I believe that he was suffering from a toothache, had lost money on the stock market and had received an angry letter from his mother."

"He told you this?"

"Not directly," Mrs Quinn said; "he mentioned these complaints to Mrs Petrie when we sat down to dinner."

"Did Charles take any medication to relieve his toothache?"

Mrs Quinn thought for a moment. She drew another circle upon her skirt. Then she said, "Charles mentioned to the doctors that he took laudanum; he rubbed it on to his gums."

That was a common practice, Daniel considered. Indeed, in the past, he had felt the need to apply laudanum to his own gums.

While frowning at Mrs Quinn, he said, "You

ordered Florrie, the maid, to obtain mustard mixed in water and a cup of coffee."

"I did," Mrs Quinn confessed. "I stirred the mustard into the water with my finger. Then I fed the mixture to Charles. However, his jaw locked and most of the mixture spilled down the front of his nightshirt."

"What of the coffee?" Daniel asked.

"Charles swallowed some of the coffee. However, immediately, he was sick into a basin."

"And what of the basin?"

"I ordered Florrie to clean it, of course."

"While you were tending Charles," Daniel said, "did you notice any medicine bottles in the bedroom?"

Mrs Quinn inclined her head. She said, "On the mantelpiece, I noticed a chloroform bottle; and, on Charles' dressing table, bottles of laudanum, ammonia and camphor compound."

"Charles' bedroom resembled a pharmacy," Daniel smiled.

"At times," Mrs Quinn replied without humour, "it did."

Changing tack, Daniel asked, "How many horses are there at the Grange?"

"Two," Mrs Quinn said. "There used to be four, when I lived there."

"What happened to the other two?"

"Charles put them down."

"Why?"

"To save money."

"Did he seek other ways to cut the household expenditure?"

Mrs Quinn turned away. She stared at the dust motes, which drifted across the room. "You must discuss that with Mrs Petrie," she murmured.

"Grace employs a groom," Daniel said.

"A new man, Pegram."

"What happened to the old groom?"

"Bert Kemp; Charles dismissed him."

"For what reason?" Daniel asked.

"Bert Kemp had an accident whilst driving Mrs Petrie in the brougham."

"How did Kemp react to his dismissal?"

"He lost his lodgings along with his job. He was very angry. I believe he said, 'Mr Petrie will not live beyond four months into the marriage.'"

"The marriage lasted four and a half months," Daniel recalled.

"That is correct."

"Nevertheless, a prophetic statement by Kemp."

Mrs Quinn smiled a secret smile, as though responding to her own amusement.

"Where does Kemp reside now?" Daniel asked.

"I believe that he secured employment with

Mrs Knight, at Merthyr Mawr."

Daniel nodded. He took a step towards the splintered door. With his right hand on the doorknob, he said, "Thank you, Mrs Quinn. You have been a great help."

The woman in black looked up. She smiled with serenity and said, "I aim to serve and please."

* * *

Daniel returned to his lodgings at the Prince of Wales Inn. There, while standing in the courtyard, he watched as the landlord rolled barrels of precious ale towards the homely inn. With the sun high in the sky, and baking the parched ground, Daniel could picture the local coalminers and agricultural workers strolling up to the inn, to drink those barrels dry.

However, before Daniel could contemplate his own thirst, Mr Robeson approached with a huge grin on his face.

"You talked with the servants," Daniel said.

"I did. All claim a great affection for Mr Petrie."

"And their stories, they rang true?"

"On the night Charles Petrie was taken ill, all the male servants remained downstairs on account of Mrs Petrie's disposition; she was dressed in her nightclothes. I detected no words of deception. I noted one or two minor inconsistencies. However, with the confusion of the evening and the passing of time, that is to be expected?"

"Their words hint at the truth," Daniel said. "If the servants had perfected their tales that would suggest collusion."

Daniel paused as a horse and cart made its sedate way towards the Grange. Then, in the middle distance, he spied the spinning wheels of a landau, with Carys Beaumond at the reins.

With his gaze fixed upon Carys, Daniel addressed Mr Robeson. He said, "One of the servants, Bert Kemp, was dismissed on the eve of the wedding. Locate him, talk with him; he labours now at Merthyr Mawr as a groom for Mrs Knight. Take our landau," Daniel instructed, "for Merthyr Mawr is close on five miles away. Also, there is a police station in Porthcawl; talk with the local constables; gather their impressions and the station gossip."

Mr Robeson nodded. He climbed aboard the landau and sped away.

With the dust from Mr Robeson's wheels clearing, Carys eased her carriage to a halt. Reaching down, she accepted Daniel's offer of a supportive hand. Then she jumped down, on to the courtyard pebbles, to join him.

"Good day, ma'am," Daniel smiled.

"Good day," Carys said. She turned to look at the labourers in the fields, at the golden hills of the sand dunes and at the landlord's scruffy dog, which had taken a fancy to an empty beer barrel.

"What brings you to the Prince of Wales?" Daniel asked.

"I was looking for you," Carys said. She smiled warmly. Then she offered her parasol a playful twirl.

"Would you care to walk and talk?" Daniel asked.

"I would find that most agreeable," Carys said, inclining her head.

They walked along a golden trail, which wound its way through the sand dunes. In the distance, Daniel spied the Grange while, straight ahead, he noticed a large freshwater pool.

"Have you made any progress?" Carys asked. Now, she held her parasol above her head, to shield her delicate features from the warm afternoon sunshine.

"A little," Daniel said.

"Do you know who poisoned Charles?"

"Not yet," he confessed.

They climbed a large sand dune and from there Daniel absorbed his surroundings. To the east, stood the Prince of Wales Inn; to the west, the coast and the freshwater pool; the Grange stood to the south-west while, three miles further south, Daniel placed the town of Porthcawl. Mr Robeson was travelling five miles south-east, to the village of Merthyr Mawr.

Secure in his bearings, Daniel turned to Carys. With their shadows merging, he asked, "What impression did you form of Charles?"

"I found him charming and likeable at times."

"And at other times?"

"He could be moody and abrupt, particularly when talk centred on money."

"Did he have a mania for money?"

Carys frowned. Deep in concentration, she bit her lower lip. Meanwhile, ahead, on the pool, a large bird prepared to land while, at her feet, a small insect burrowed into the sand. While admiring the sinuous trail left by the insect, Carys said, "During one of our conversations, Grace confessed that Charles did have a mania for money."

"Did he have a temper?"

"A very quick temper," Carys said. "On one occasion, he displayed his bad humour in front of me and, I have to confess, I was frightened at the time."

"Charles sacked a groom, Bert Kemp."

Carys inclined her head. Then she accepted Daniel's offer of a helping hand as they negotiated an area of undulating, uneven ground.

"Charles and Kemp had a big falling out," Carys said. "Charles accused Kemp of careless driving, of damaging the brougham; in turn, Kemp spoke his mind, in heated terms."

"Surely," Daniel frowned, "it is unusual for a servant to speak his mind?"

"Kemp always spoke his mind," Carys said.

Daniel turned to the south-west, to gaze at the Grange. The building looked large in its isolation, pleasant in the sunlight. However, he wondered at its ambience in the midst of a stormy night.

"The Grange covers a large estate," Daniel said; "Grace must employ a number of staff to run that estate."

"Eight household staff," Carys said, "plus three gardeners, a coachman and a groom. However, a month before he died, Charles dismissed two of the gardeners and two of the household staff."

"For what reason?" Daniel asked.

"To save money, I believe."

"And yet," Daniel reasoned, "through Grace, Charles had more money than he would ever spend."

"Charles was very parsimonious," Carys said; "he detested waste and accused Grace of being frivolous with her money."

"Did the sacked household staff and gardeners

offer words of protest?"

"If they did," Carys said, "those words did not reach my ears."

Daniel and Carys walked on in pleasant harmony, until they arrived at the freshwater pool. Daniel gazed at the pool, into the clear, inviting water. A strong swimmer, he contemplated diving into the pool; however, not today – maybe on another occasion.

"What of Mrs Quinn," Daniel asked; "after the wedding, her position must have been tenuous?"

"By your words," Carys said, "do you suggest that a married woman has no need of a lady's companion?"

"I daresay," Daniel said, "that a married woman could still take pleasure in talking with her companion; however, does she really need that companion to sit at the dinner table and share in the intimate moments of the day?"

Carys thought for a moment. She gave her parasol a playful twirl. Whenever she lapsed into deep thought, Daniel noticed, her face became serious. However, her sanguine nature soon produced a smile and the sunshine within that smile swept the clouds away.

"I believe that Charles talked of dismissing Mrs Quinn," Carys said. "On one occasion, Grace told me that, initially, she employed Mrs Quinn at £80 per annum; however, her salary rose to £100 in the fourth year."

"That is four times the salary of a maid," Daniel said.

"It is a generous sum," Carys agreed.

"Furthermore, it is a lot of money to lose; I imagine that Mrs Quinn would find it difficult to secure a similar well-paid position."

Carys glanced over her shoulder. She lowered her parasol until it shielded her face. Then, in a conspiratorial whisper, she said, "Do you suspect Mrs Quinn of administering the poison?"

"I suspect no one," Daniel smiled, "and yet, I suspect everyone."

Carys scowled. She raised her parasol and gave it a vigorous twirl. "That is an evasive answer," she complained.

"I am an advocate," Daniel laughed; "evasion is an essential tool of my trade."

Daniel and Carys walked on in easy silence, past the tall reeds, which fringed the northern sector of the pool. The reeds looked attractive, Daniel noted. However, they would be dangerous for swimmers.

"Grace has few friends," Daniel said.

"That is true," Carys agreed. "Because of the scandal, which surrounded her first marriage, many people shun her."

"But not you."

"Maybe people shun me too," Carys said; she offered Daniel a coquettish smile, "and, like Grace, I am in need of a friend."

"I do not believe that for one moment," Daniel said, his tone light, friendly. He walked on. Then, after a pause for reflection, he added, "As a friend, you must have noticed that Grace consumes sherry way beyond her basic needs."

Carys inclined her head then said, "Grace confessed that her consumption is a habit born of her first marriage; she imbibed copious amounts of sherry when Gustav beat her; now she drinks to calm her nerves."

"Did Charles drink?" Daniel asked.

"He drank burgundy," Carys said, "and brandy, but not to excess."

"Did Charles complain of Grace's nervous disposition?"

"I believe he did. I believe it caused him some distress."

Daniel paused to consider Carys' answer. Then he said, "Has Grace sought help to cure her nervous disposition?"

Carys nodded. She said, "Before her marriage to Charles, Grace visited Dr Collymore at Newton. He administers the spa on Newton Beach."

"Dr Collymore..." Daniel searched his mind for

references to the physician; according to newspaper reports, his patients held him in high esteem. "I understand," Daniel said, "that Dr Collymore is a man with a fine reputation."

"In the field of hydropathic treatments," Carys said, "Dr Collymore is regarded as the finest physician."

Daniel smiled. "Then I shall talk with Dr Collymore."

Once again, Carys inclined her head. Then she led Daniel on to the well-worn track, and they walked back to the inn.

At the inn, when seated in her landau, Carys turned to Daniel and said, "Mr Morgan..." She paused to draw in a deep breath. "Would you, and Mr Robeson of course, do me the honour of dining at my table tomorrow night?"

"That would be our pleasure," Daniel said. He bowed in gracious fashion. "Thank you for the invitation."

Carys exhaled. With a sigh of relief, she said, "Then we shall meet again, tomorrow night."

* * *

With Dr Collymore in mind, Daniel walked to Newton. It was a beautiful day, he considered, and he felt in need of the exercise.

Natural springs flowed in abundance within the local landscape. Dr Collymore had taken advantage of those springs, in particular, the water that flowed from St John's Well on to nearby Newton Beach. There, on the beach, he had established an open-air spa, complete with a large stone slab. The slab served as a dispensing post, a natural counter for his homeopathic medicines.

As Daniel walked the two miles to Newton, he reflected upon his knowledge of Dr James Onesiphorus Collymore. Born in 1808, the doctor was sixty-eight years old. He counted travel, literature, opera, nature and spiritualism amongst his hobbies.

Daniel's memory suggested that the doctor's ancestors had made a small fortune through coffee in the West Indies. Suitably financed, the young James Collymore had studied medicine in Paris. Later, he had travelled around Europe paying close attention to the various techniques employed at numerous health spas.

Rich in experience and knowledge, Dr Collymore vowed to establish his own spa. Upon chance, while visiting a friend in Newton, he learned about the local springs and their healing properties. Immediately, he developed a health spa and, within five years, the rich, the famous and the fashionable were flocking to take to his waters.

Daniel arrived at Dr Collymore's clinic, an impressive Georgian building with a rich, red blush within its fine stone. There, he enquired at the servants' entrance and through the auspices of Pritchard, Dr Collymore's butler, was granted admission to the doctor's consulting room, a room equipped with a marble fireplace, numerous bookshelves and a large oak desk. Parchment and inks littered the desk, under the shadow of a lamp and its moon-like globe. Daniel also noticed paintings, presumably copies, by Carlo Dolci and Fra Angelico. The greens and browns of the room were offset by a display of brass and silver ornaments, and by a splendid ormolu clock.

When Dr Collymore entered the consulting room his stature took Daniel by surprise, for he was a short, rotund man, clean-shaven with ruddy cheeks. His head was bald, save for a neat silvery corona, while a pince-nez enhanced his intelligent blue eyes.

"Daniel Morgan," Daniel said, "advocate; I shall speak for Grace Petrie at the forthcoming inquest into the death of Charles Petrie. I would be grateful to sit with you and discuss matters relating to Mrs Petrie's health."

"She is aware of your presence in my consulting room?" Dr Collymore frowned.

"Mrs Petrie has granted me *carte blanche*,"

Daniel said. "If the inquest goes against her, she faces a charge of murder and, beyond that, the hangman's rope."

"I see," Dr Collymore said. "In that case, you had better sit down."

The two men made themselves comfortable at Dr Collymore's desk; the doctor sat behind the desk, while Daniel sat on a soft leather chair.

"Would you care for a cup of cold tea?" Dr Collymore asked.

"Cold tea?" Daniel smiled.

"Yes, I believe that all drinks are best served cold."

"Therefore," Daniel said, "it would please me to join you."

Dr Collymore bowed. He stood and walked towards the window wall. There, he pulled on a silken sash. Within seconds, Pritchard, the butler, appeared at the consulting room door; after twenty years of service, he had learned how to predict his master's behaviour.

"Two cold teas, please," Dr Collymore said and, with silent tread, Pritchard retreated from the consulting room.

"Your spa," Daniel ventured, "it treats patients through hydropathy?"

"Hydropathy and homeopathy," Dr Collymore said. He placed his hands together, as though in prayer. Then he eased his fingers against his chin. "All chronic disease stems from the fact that the viscera is starved of blood, or engorged with blood; therefore, cold water applied to the skin, through various methods, stimulates the circulation and thus cures the morbid condition or, at the very least, checks and relieves the symptoms. I place my patients in sodden sheets, for several hours at a time. They also undergo douches, lateral and horizontal showers, cold baths, sitz-baths, foot-baths, plunge-baths and sessions in the sea. When necessary, I apply cold compresses. Furthermore, all my patients drink copious amounts of spring water."

"Did you apply these treatments to Mrs Petrie," Daniel asked, "in regard to her nervous condition?"

"Indeed," Dr Collymore said, "I applied my therapies to Grace, and they were a great success."

Dr Collymore referred to Grace as 'Grace', and not 'Mrs Petrie', Daniel noted; just as Mrs Quinn had referred to Charles Petrie as 'Charles'; in terms of masters and servants, there appeared to be a great familiarity at the Grange.

"Mrs Petrie has a passion for sherry," Daniel said.

Dr Collymore removed his pince-nez. Upon a soft cloth, he polished each lens. "My therapies cured Grace of that passion," he said.

"However," Daniel said, "she is drinking heavily again."

Dr Collymore looked up and Daniel noticed a heavy sadness in his eyes. "That is to be lamented," the doctor said.

"Mrs Petrie has not asked for your help again?"

"She has not," Dr Collymore said.

A steady rapping on the consulting room door brought a temporary halt to the conversation. Dr Collymore said, "Enter," and Pritchard stepped into the room. Upon the doctor's desk, he placed a silver tray laden with a china tea service. Then he retreated with a low bow of his head.

As Dr Collymore poured the cold tea into two stylish teacups, Daniel said, "Over the three days that Charles Petrie lay in agony, six doctors were called, but not you."

"That is because I am no longer welcome at the Grange," Dr Collymore said, "not since the wedding."

"For what reason?" Daniel asked.

The doctor placed his teapot on the tray. Then he handed a china teacup to Daniel, who accepted the drink with a word of thanks.

"Mr Petrie disapproved of my methods," Dr Collymore said; "he felt that he was better qualified to tend to Grace."

"But," Daniel said, "he was not a doctor."

Dr Collymore placed his pince-nez on a speckled blotter. He studied the blotter. Then he reached for his teacup. After sipping his tea, he said, "I understand that Mr Petrie took an interest in medicine, and that he had friends in the medical profession."

"What sort of interest?"

"He had a fondness for observing operations."

"What of his other interests?" Daniel asked.

"I am sorry," Dr Collymore said, "I cannot help you; I never met the man."

"Not even in town, or out walking?"

Dr Collymore offered an indifferent shrug of his right shoulder. He said, "Mr Petrie was in the habit of looking the other way."

Daniel nodded. He sipped his tea. In truth, in recent years, he had spent too much time in coffeehouses developing a taste for coffee; tea, hot or cold, failed to stir his taste buds.

Nevertheless, Daniel offered respect to his host. He sipped his tea. Then he said, "I understand that Charles Petrie was a banker and keen to enter politics."

Once again, Dr Collymore offered a casual shrug of his right shoulder. He said, "You are better informed than I am, sir."

Daniel placed his teacup on its saucer. After a moment's thought, he decided on a change of tack.

"Do you live alone, Dr Collymore?"

"I live with my two sisters; they keep house for me."

"Are your sisters at home?"

"They are not," Dr Collymore said; "they are out, visiting a friend."

"Forgive me for this confusion," Daniel said, "but I believe that certain newspaper reports offered reference to your wife?"

"My first wife died thirty-eight years ago," Dr Collymore said. "My second wife is older than me, by some seventeen years. She is of feeble mind and is housed in an institution."

"I am sorry," Daniel said. He drained his teacup, save for the dregs. Sitting back, he asked, "When did you first apply your hydropathic treatments to Grace?"

"That was during her first marriage, at the tail end of that marriage."

"Therefore," Daniel said, "you have known Grace for some time."

"I knew her as a child," Dr Collymore said, "for a brief time. However, we only met again in recent years, when she felt strained by her first marriage."

"Her first husband, Gustav, died of alcohol poisoning. Did you treat him?"

"No," Dr Collymore said, "he never sought my cure."

Daniel stood. He bowed his head. "Thank you, sir, for your time."

"Not at all," Dr Collymore said. "I am only too pleased to help."

Daniel walked to the consulting room door. There, he paused to glance over his shoulder. "One more question," he said; "are you familiar with antimony?"

Dr Collymore stared at his blotter. His fingers, suddenly nervous, reached for his pince-nez. "Antimony is a drug of my acquaintance, yes."

"Once again," Daniel said, "I thank you for your time."

\* \* \*

With the afternoon drifting into early evening, and with the labourers walking in from the fields, Daniel strolled back to his lodgings. There, in the courtyard, he met Mr Robeson.

"Bert Kemp refused to talk with me," Mr Robeson said, "on account of my dusky complexion."

Daniel scowled then said, "A bigot for breakfast; first thing in the morning, we shall have words with Bert Kemp."

Mr Robeson smiled then nodded. "However," he said, "with a jug of ale in their hands, the local constables were more forthcoming. They told me that Mary Petrie informed them of her suspicions on the 1st May. Seven days later, they conducted a search of the Grange and its stables. During that search, they found a number of medicine bottles. They removed the bottles for analysis, but no traces of antimony were found. On that same date, the 8th May, a reward of £500 leading to an arrest was placed in the local newspaper. No one stepped forward to claim that reward."

"Do the police have any suspects?" Daniel asked.

"I spoke with five constables, and each offered a different opinion. Each opinion was based on hearsay, none on fact. The police have no clue; we shall obtain no joy there."

Daniel inclined his head. With a firm hand, he slapped his companion upon his broad back. "You, sir, have earned your reward."

"A glass of fine wine?" Mr Robeson ventured, his smile wide and sanguine.

"On my account," Daniel said.

## August 13th 1876

After breakfast, Daniel sent a telegram to Professor Vernon Pennington, an expert on poisons, a senior physician who had tended Charles Petrie during his three days of torment. In the telegram, Daniel explained his interest and requested a meeting, to discuss aspects of the case.

Then, with Mr Robeson at the reins, Daniel travelled five miles south-east, to visit Bert Kemp. He travelled in the rented landau, which made good speed over the dry and dusty roads.

Mr Robeson eased the horses to a trot as they traversed a humpbacked bridge. The bridge straddled a wide river, which flowed in lazy fashion through trees and fields, through woodland and farmland, through sand dunes to the sea.

Amongst the thatched cottages of Merthyr Mawr, within the tiny hamlet, Daniel located the farm owned by Mrs Knight. There, in the stables, he found Bert Kemp.

A robust man in his mid-thirties, Bert Kemp possessed a rich mane of black hair, combed back to form a widow's peak. His dark eyes were deep-set in a full, round face, a face distinguished by its swarthy appearance and by a series of pockmarks upon his chin.

"Mr Kemp?" Daniel enquired.

"And who might you be?"

"Daniel Morgan, advocate. Mr Robeson, I believe you have already met."

Kemp glared at Daniel and Mr Robeson. Then he wiped his hands on the front of his grey flannel shirt.

"You worked for Mrs Grace Petrie," Daniel said.

"Aye," Kemp agreed, "for three years."

"And before that?"

"I worked for Dr Collymore."

Daniel smiled. "It is indeed a small world."

"The doctor recommended my services to Mrs Petrie."

"Therefore, this period of employment was after Gustav, Mrs Petrie's first husband, had died."

"Indeed, it was," Kemp agreed.

"I understand that Charles Petrie sacked you on the eve of the wedding."

"He did."

"For what reason?"

"He blamed me for damaging the brougham, but it wasn't my fault. The other driver drove into us, but he wouldn't accept the blame."

"By 'us'," Daniel said, "you refer to yourself and Mrs Petrie?"

"I do."

"I understand that you displayed anger at your

dismissal."

"I was very annoyed," Kemp confessed.

"I understand that you exchanged hot words with Mr Petrie."

"I exchanged hot words," Kemp said, "but not with him."

"If not with him," Daniel asked, "then with whom?"

"With the landlord at the Prince of Wales Inn."

"What did you say to the landlord?"

"I told him that Mr Petrie would not live beyond four months into the marriage."

"He lived four months and two weeks into the marriage." Daniel smiled then asked, "Are you a soothsayer, or a groomsman, Mr Kemp?"

"I am a horseman," Kemp said, "pure and simple."

As though to prove his statement, Kemp turned to tend a fine, proud carthorse, his calloused fingers caressing the animal's mane. Meanwhile, the carthorse flicked its tail and eyed Daniel through world-weary eyes. Flies occupied the stables and many of them displayed an interest in the carthorse. However, the handsome beast merely blinked or swished its tail.

"I understand that grooms use antimony," Daniel said.

"True," Kemp replied, his tone curt, his

expression grim.

"For what purpose?"

"To worm the horses, and to clear their coats of sores."

"Do you use antimony?" Daniel asked.

"I do," Kemp said.

"Do you use white antimony or liver of antimony?"

"I use white antimony," Kemp said.

Daniel inclined his head. He turned to Mr Robeson and the two men exchanged a knowing look.

To Kemp, Daniel said, "I believe that the majority of grooms use liver of antimony."

"That's for them," Kemp replied, his tone brusque.

"Charles Petrie was poisoned with white antimony, tartar emetic."

The groom shrugged. He said, "I had no hand in that."

Kemp paused. He glared at Daniel and Mr Robeson. Then he walked out of the stables, into the yard. In the yard, a young dog followed a random scent, while doves, four in number, perched on a shed roof. The roof was tiled and bowed in the middle, with the central tiles discoloured through the channelling of rain.

"Where do you purchase your antimony?"

Daniel asked.

"From the pharmacy," Kemp said; "I sign the register."

"When was the last time you purchased antimony?"

"I can't help you," Kemp said; "my mind's a perfect blank."

The young dog ran around the yard. Then he paused to sniff Mr Robeson's shoes. In keeping with his general appearance, Mr Robeson's shoes were immaculate, a symbol of style. Meanwhile, Kemp removed a leather apron from a fence post and tied it around his waist. Suitably attired, he returned to the stables.

"Did you use antimony at the Grange?" Daniel asked.

Kemp nodded. "I did."

"And what of the excess; did you dispose of it, after your dismissal?"

"Without doubt," Kemp said; "I poured it down the drain."

"Did anyone witness that act?"

From over his right shoulder, Kemp offered Daniel a sly look. Then he squatted beside the carthorse. While examining the horse's hind legs, he said, "Someone might have seen me; I'm not sure; I can't help you; my mind's a perfect blank."

Daniel turned to go. He would talk with Kemp

again, under oath, at the inquest; maybe the presence of a coroner and a jury would restore the groom's memory. On the other hand, if he had something to hide, he might retreat further into his shell.

Satisfied with the horse's health, Kemp straightened. Then, from a corner of the stables, he picked up a bando stick and ran a finger along its length.

"A man is judged by the company he keeps," Kemp said, pointing the bando stick at Mr Robeson.

"Do you object to the company I keep?" Daniel asked, his tone even, polite.

Kemp glared at Mr Robeson. Through clenched teeth, he said, "We have no call for the likes of him around here."

Responding to the fetid atmosphere, the horse whinnied, and Kemp followed suit. With a laugh, the groom said, "Look, he's making the horse nervous."

"Your fear of Mr Robeson is making the horse nervous," Daniel said. "I should relax, and place that bando stick in a safe place, if I were you."

"I don't fear him," Kemp said. He turned and spat on the straw.

"In that case," Daniel said, "you can add imprudence to your ignorance. I wish you good day. I will see you in court."

*  *  *

Daniel and Mr Robeson returned to the Prince of Wales Inn to find a telegram waiting for them. Professor Vernon Pennington had replied post-haste; he would meet Daniel to discuss his findings into Charles Petrie's poisoning. The telegram concluded, 'Please travel to my home in St Hilary at your earliest convenience.'

Situated fifteen miles to the east of Sker Grange, St Hilary was a small village, a home to a hundred and sixty people, most of them agricultural labourers and rural craftsmen. Nevertheless, St Hilary could also boast a number of fine manor houses, and Professor Vernon Pennington resided in one of them, a sprawling two-storey mansion with a long veranda and a number of large ornate windows. A previous generation had bricked up two of the first floor windows to evade the gentry-despised Window Tax, introduced in 1696 and repealed a hundred and fifty-five years later.

In the landau, and while pausing at regular waterholes to refresh the horses, Daniel made his way to St Hilary. In his absence, Mr Robeson gathered intelligence from the locals at the inn.

As he travelled, Daniel reflected on Professor Pennington's background. An eminent physician, and an expert on poisons, the professor had treated many notable individuals. Indeed, he was widely regarded as the leading medical man in the county.

Daniel eased the landau to a halt. From his seated position, he peered over a privet hedge to a lush green lawn. Three young men, the professor's sons, played croquet on the lawn, while his wife and daughter looked on. The ladies laughed, sipped lemonade and entertained the family dog, a lively springer spaniel. Meanwhile, the professor caught sight of Daniel. He spoke to his wife. Then he strode with purpose towards the porch to greet him.

Tall and erect, Professor Vernon Pennington possessed dark hair, parted in the centre. His eyes were dark and solemn while slim side-whiskers framed a long, sullen face. He looked imperious in a formal frock coat, fashioned from a fine worsted cloth. The tailor had applied the same black cloth to the professor's trousers, while a white shirt, a butterfly collar and a black bow tie completed his ensemble.

"Professor Pennington," Daniel smiled. He bowed in greeting.

"Mr Morgan, I presume," the professor replied, his voice as dark as the grave. "Please," he said, "step into my library."

Daniel followed the professor into a room rich in mahogany furniture and plentiful in books.

Indeed, books lined three of the walls, while a large bay window occupied the fourth wall. A huge desk sat under the window. The desk offered a view of two impressive globes positioned with precision on two iron stands. A number of photographs also decorated the room, which suggested an interest in the current fashion of photography.

Professor Pennington sat behind his desk while Daniel sat on a firm wooden chair. The desk contained a number of medical instruments, which looked gruesome to the untutored eye.

"I wish to talk with you about Charles Petrie's poisoning," Daniel said. "I believe that you tended Mr Petrie, on the second day of his illness."

The professor pursed his lips. He narrowed his eyes. Then, after great deliberation, he said, "Five other doctors were also in attendance. However, Mrs Petrie did ask for my opinion."

"How did you find him?" Daniel asked.

"I found Charles Petrie in a great deal of distress. He was totally unconscious, with his pupils dilated; his skin was cold and his breathing was irregular; I had difficulty in locating a pulse; to be blunt, the man was heart dead and ready to meet his Maker."

Daniel frowned. "Heart dead?"

"A turn of phrase," Professor Pennington said; "life had all but departed the body."

"Did Charles vomit in your presence?" Daniel asked.

"He did. And he passed matter through his back passage. Both acts were uncontrolled."

"Did you suspect poison at that stage?"

Professor Pennington placed his hands together. He steepled his fingers, to form a pyramid above his desk. The professor possessed large hands, Daniel noted, and long fingers with squared-off fingernails. Gravely, he intoned, "Poison seemed the most likely explanation for the poor man's symptoms."

"Later," Daniel said, "you conducted a post mortem."

The professor offered a gentle inclination of his head and said, "Yes, I did."

"And the post mortem confirmed your suspicions?"

"Yes, it did."

"What quantity of antimony did you find in Charles Petrie's body?"

"Approximately twenty grains. I found twenty grains; however, I estimate that the man swallowed forty grains; the remainder passed through his system as vomit, etcetera."

"Twenty or forty," Daniel said, "either quantity sounds like a large dose."

"An extremely large dose," Professor

Pennington said. "Ten grains of antimony would kill a man."

"As a result," Daniel surmised, "the person who supplied the antimony intended to kill Charles."

"That is one conclusion," Professor Pennington said.

"You have reached another conclusion?"

"I have," he intoned. "However, I will reserve my opinion for the inquest."

Daniel paused and reflected upon the professor's words. Through the bay window, he noticed a butterfly as it swooped down, only to rise and disappear into the air. Meanwhile, above his head, a large crystal chandelier swayed slightly, disturbed by a gentle breeze. For some reason, Daniel pictured the crystal chandelier as the Sword of Damocles, and he wondered upon whom it was about to fall.

Professor Pennington coughed politely, and Daniel offered him his full attention. With his gaze fixed upon the medical man, he said, "Sir, could you please enlighten a layman as to antimony and its properties?"

"Antimony is a metallic element," Professor Pennington said. "Its compounds are used in ceramics, dyestuffs, enamels and glass. As tartar emetic, you will also find antimony in a range of medicines. People have used these medicines for centuries without distress or undue alarm."

"Thank you," Daniel said. "Now, could you please tell me, how did the antimony enter Charles Petrie's body?"

"One possibility is through food."

"Is that likely?" Daniel asked.

"In my opinion, no," the professor said, his face stern, his tone laden with a learned conviction.

"How so?"

"Because food would not disguise the taste of tartar emetic."

"Charles drank burgundy with his final meal."

"If someone placed antimony into a glass of burgundy," Professor Pennington said, "the chemical would cloud the claret. Unless a man was extremely drunk, or of simple mind, he would notice the difference."

"Water?" Daniel ventured. "Could the murderer have poisoned Charles through a simple, occasional drink?"

"Water seems a more likely source," the professor agreed.

"Antimony dissolves in water?"

"It does. Furthermore, it loses its taste."

"Aside from the antimony," Daniel asked, "did you find any disagreeable elements within Charles Petrie's body, arsenic, for example?"

"Initially," the professor said, "I suspected arsenic, but I found no trace of that substance. However, I did discover a trace of laudanum; I understand that the man complained of a toothache and applied an excessive amount of laudanum to his gums."

"Could the laudanum have killed him?" Daniel asked.

"The antimony killed him," Professor Pennington said; "of that, I have no doubt."

Daniel stood. He bowed towards the professor. "Thank you, sir."

"My pleasure," Professor Pennington said. "I shall walk with you, to your landau."

In the garden, Daniel noticed that three young women had joined the three young men, presumably their wives or fiancées. The young men were instructing the young women upon the finer arts of croquet, amidst great laughter.

As Professor Pennington and Daniel strolled through the garden, the medical man turned and smiled at the croquet scene. However, the smile seemed alien to his lips and pained his expression.

At the landau, the professor said, "Towards the end, Charles Petrie became lucid. Furthermore, when I pressed him about the laudanum, I am convinced that he had something on his mind. He maintained that he had taken laudanum and nothing else. I explained that laudanum would not have produced his symptoms. However, he ignored me and insisted that we should offer up prayers."

"Which you did?"

"Charles Petrie offered up the Lord's Prayer," Professor Pennington said, "which I intoned."

"Willingly?"

"I am a man of science; I do not have a great faith in religion. Nevertheless, I acquiesced to his dying wish."

"Charles knew that he was dying?"

"I made that plain. I felt as though it was my duty."

"Yet," Daniel said, "he offered no explanation or accusation?"

"Charles Petrie had something on his mind," Professor Pennington said. "However, for some reason, the words would not pass from his lips."

* * *

From St Hilary, Daniel returned to his lodgings at the Prince of Wales Inn. With light evening clouds offering a pink tint to the sky, Daniel retired to his room. There, he discarded his day clothes and prepared for the evening meal at Beaumond Hall. Daniel displayed a preference for bohemian fashion. Therefore, he concluded that his velvet jacket and silk shirt would complement the evening.

Daniel was straightening his jacket when Mr Robeson knocked upon his door. "Enter," Daniel said, and the proud Nevisian walked in.

"Someone to see you," Mr Robeson said. "A fellow advocate."

"His name?" Daniel asked.

"Mr Lewis Murdoch."

"Advocate for Mary, Charles Petrie's mother. We shall meet, within the inn."

Daniel found Lewis Murdoch in an alcove, nursing a glass of brandy. He sat at a wooden table, an item of furniture that looked decidedly older than the building.

"Mr Morgan," Lewis Murdoch smiled as Daniel approached.

"At your service, sir."

"My name is Lewis Murdoch; I am the advocate for Mr Charles Petrie's family."

"Specifically," Daniel said, "you are the advocate for Mary, Charles' mother."

"Indeed, sir; would you care to join me in a glass of brandy?"

"I shall sit with you," Daniel said. "However, I will reserve the brandy for later in the evening."

Daniel eased on to a bench, opposite Lewis Murdoch. From his seated position, he appraised his fellow advocate, and forthcoming rival. In his early forties, Murdoch possessed wavy blond hair, swept back from his forehead. Of small build, his features displayed a long thin nose and a heavy, unkempt moustache. His eyes were small, like gimlets, and set close together. He wore baggy trousers, a long morning coat and a double-breasted waistcoat. In addition, the collar on his shirt was narrow and stiff, while his bow tie held its own opinion, hanging skew-whiff. A further item caught Daniel's attention, a monocle, which Murdoch sported over his right eye.

"You know of me?" Lewis Murdoch asked, as though inviting a compliment.

"I do," Daniel said; "I have observed you at work."

"Then, sir, you will be aware that I always win the day." Murdoch raised his brandy glass and offered a toast, to victory. Indeed, his confident manner suggested that a verdict, of murder, was already assured.

"Surely," Daniel said, "the forthcoming inquest is not about winning or losing; it is about establishing the truth."

"I shall establish the truth," Murdoch said, "for truth and justice are always on my side."

He paused to adjust his monocle, and to glare at a group of boisterous agricultural workers who had strolled into the inn to slake their thirsts.

"A word of advice..." Murdoch leaned forward. He lowered his voice to a conspiratorial whisper. "In matters of this sort, it is always best if the truth emerges quickly; the longer these inquests drag on, the more scandal they are likely to expose."

"You anticipate scandal?" Daniel asked, raising an inquisitive eyebrow.

"I do not anticipate," Murdoch said, "I know."

"You have a good source?"

Murdoch smiled and the bristles on his unkempt moustache, now soaked in brandy, twitched. "Indeed, sir, I have a very reliable source; someone familiar with Grace Petrie and her household."

"Would you care to name that source?" Daniel asked, his tone playful.

"And allow you an advantage." Murdoch sat back. He laughed, "Sir, do you take me for a fool?"

"You seek a quick verdict," Daniel said.

Murdoch slurped and spilled his brandy. He licked his lips while a rich rivulet of the fermented fruit juice ran along the table. "If the inquest lasts one day," he paused to suppress a burp, "or one hundred days, my fee is assured."

"And a royal fee at that," Daniel said, "I feel certain."

Daniel knew Lewis Murdoch and his like all too well. Many of them had made a small fortune from railway, coal and iron contracts – honest work, a legitimate endeavour. However, from a position of strength, some advocates now overcharged their clients, their search for the truth blinded by the glint of silver and the glitter of gold. A quick verdict in the Charles Petrie inquest and Lewis Murdoch would move on to pocket another hefty fee. From the number of witnesses listed, he had calculated the length of the inquest, doubled that number and charged his client accordingly.

"You will push for a verdict of murder," Daniel said.

"It is the natural and correct course. And in most cases of domestic murder, who is the culprit?"

"The spouse," Daniel said.

Lewis Murdoch smiled. He sipped his brandy then nodded in sagacious fashion.

"You suspect Grace Petrie of murder?"

"I do not suspect," Murdoch said. "I know." Once again, he leaned forward and lowered his voice to a conspiratorial whisper. "A confession would save a great deal of anguish; if Grace Petrie were to confess, it would avert a lot of pain."

"A confession would lead to the hangman," Daniel said.

"Indeed," Lewis Murdoch smiled. "However, surely it is better to meet with the hangman than to reveal your darkest secrets in public."

* * *

Beaumond Hall dated from the twelfth century when the Norman invaders established a manor house in the village of Corneli. Redeveloped and rebuilt over the years, Beaumond Hall contained few of its medieval features, although a knowing eye could still spy medieval masonry within the boundary walls.

With a glorious August sunset at their backs, Daniel and Mr Robeson walked two miles inland, from the Prince of Wales Inn to Beaumond Hall. At the Hall, an expectant Carys Beaumond stepped forward to greet them. She looked splendid in a one-piece, front-buttoning Princess dress. The gold silk of the dress perfectly suited Carys' slender frame, its outline clearly defining her femininity.

"Mr Morgan, Mr Robeson," Carys enthused, "you are most welcome. Pray, enter the library; dinner will be served within the half hour."

Daniel and Mr Robeson followed Carys into her library. Rich autumnal shades dominated the library, along with hundreds of books, numerous paintings and a selection of photographs. In particular, a photograph depicting Carys and a man several years her senior attracted Daniel's attention.

"A distinguished looking gentleman," Daniel

said.

"Hopkin, my late husband," Carys said with some affection. "He was considerably older than me and unwell before our marriage. Later, he developed tuberculosis. Although it pained me greatly, I nursed him until his final day. He was a kind man," she added with a sigh, "and it was a good marriage."

Carys invited Daniel and Mr Robeson to sit on a luxurious red sofa, the curvature of its arms and back inspired by Viennese craftsmen.

When suitably seated on an adjacent armchair, Carys continued, "I was the runt of the litter, you see; my parents had me late in life; I was the baby of nine. My parents desired that I should marry before they passed on. One day, Hopkin called at Penllan, our family home, and we discovered that we shared an interest in books. Immediately, my parents sensed a good match and, thankfully, Hopkin consented. He bequeathed me this impressive collection." She glanced around the library then waved a hand at the scores of leather-bound books. "Currently, I am translating Old Welsh texts from the Arthurian Age into English."

Carys paused to respond to Daniel's expression. With a frown, she said, "You smile, Mr Morgan. Do you think that a life devoted to books is a frivolous waste of a lady's time?"

"On the contrary," Daniel said. "I think a life devoted to books is an excellent use of a lady's time, and I look forward to reading the fruits of your labours. I smiled because your words pleased me."

"Thank you, sir." With her eyes wide, Carys' delicate features mirrored Daniel's smile. Unable to contain her excitement, her skin took on a healthy, rosy glow. "Your company pleases me," she said, "and yours too, Mr Robeson."

"You are not troubled by the colour of my skin?" Mr Robeson asked politely.

"You do not judge a man by the colour of his skin," Carys said, "or by his age, for that matter. You judge a man by the purity within his heart and the goodness within his soul."

Carys paused to acknowledge her maid, Christiana, who had appeared at the library door. Dinner was served. Therefore, Carys jumped to her feet and said, "Now, please, gentlemen accompany me into the dining room."

In the dining room, Carys, Daniel and Mr Robeson sat at a long oak table. Candelabras lit the table while fresh fruit added a touch of natural colour. The fruit also offered a vibrant contrast to the cream of the lace tablecloth.

The small party dined on a scrumptious meal of hare soup, oyster patties and Cotelettes a la Maintenon, followed by boiled turkey, mashed potatoes, stewed seakale and saddles of mutton. The dinner concluded with cabinet pudding, jaune mange, punch jelly and a cheese fondue.

Well and truly sated, Daniel sat back. He wiped his lips upon a napkin then said, "That was delicious; thank you."

In response, Carys inclined her head and smiled.

"Most excellent, Mrs Beaumond," Mr Robeson said, nodding his approval.

"Carys, please," the hostess said. "I am Carys amongst friends."

After the meal, with wine glasses in their hands, the trio retired to the drawing room. There, Daniel spied a Broadwood piano encased in black and gold. "That is a beautiful instrument," he said; "and I believe that you play?"

"You remembered," Carys smiled, "the day we first met; Christiana's search for sheet music in Cardiff. She located a number of works by Chopin; shall I entertain you?"

"We insist," Daniel and Mr Robeson said in unison. Then they settled back and listened to the Nocturnes.

"You play beautifully," Daniel said after the final note had floated away on the warm night air.

"You are too kind," Carys blushed; "in truth, I play with two left hands."

"Maybe Mr Robeson would like to accompany you," Daniel suggested while grinning at his friend.

"Yes, please." Carys clapped her hands together in excited fashion. She turned to face Mr Robeson. "Do you sing?" she asked. "I would love to hear you sing."

Mr Robeson offered a bashful shrug, rolled his shoulders then smiled. He stood beside Carys at the piano and, in a rich baritone, he sang 'Woodman, Spare that Tree', a song in praise of nature.

"That was wonderful," Carys sighed. "You have such a wonderful voice." She turned to Daniel and said, "Truly, Mr Morgan, Mr Robeson has such a wonderful voice."

"Daniel," the advocate smiled. "If you are Carys, I am Daniel."

"Daniel," she agreed. "And what of Mr Robeson?" she asked.

"Mr Robeson is Mr Robeson and we shall remain content in that knowledge."

Mr Robeson nodded his acknowledgement while Carys accepted Daniel's words without further query.

Meanwhile, Carys' fingers skipped lightly over the piano keys. She turned to Mr Robeson and said, "Please, sing for me again."

On this occasion, Mr Robeson sang 'Land of My Fathers' while Carys accompanied him on the piano. Upon reaching the chorus, Daniel joined in and the song concluded amidst peals of joy and laughter.

Sitting back, Carys wiped tears of mirth from her eyes. Then she said, "I have not enjoyed myself so much since my wedding day. You are delightful companions and you have made this a very special day." She raised her wine glass and offered a toast. "Tomorrow you will speak for Grace at the inquest, and I feel sure that you will speak well. To a successful outcome."

"To a successful outcome," Mr Robeson echoed.

"To Grace," Daniel said.

In the landau, and with Mr Robeson at the reins, Daniel, Grace and Carys arrived at the Seabank Hotel in Porthcawl at ten o'clock the following morning.

Overlooking the sea, the Seabank Hotel began life in 1860 as the New House. Ten years later, a larger house developed on the site. Soon, moss covered the outer walls, smothering the grey stone and encircling the French windows. For Daniel, two features stood out – a quaint, colourful garden at the front of the hotel and a prominent Italianate tower.

Mr Robeson eased the landau to a halt. Then, with Daniel's right hand offering support, Grace stepped down from the carriage. However, despite Daniel's firm hand, Grace's knees buckled and she paused to compose herself.

"Are you all right?" Daniel asked.

"I...I think so," Grace hesitated. She glanced towards the hotel, which the authorities had commissioned as the venue for the inquest.

A large crowd had gathered outside the hotel, all well heeled and fashionable; the labourers were toiling in the fields, the coalminers sweating underground, the quarrymen wiping dust from their faces. However, for those with time on their hands, and a guaranteed income, the inquest was the hottest ticket in town. Indeed, many had travelled from outside the town to view the drama.

"You have told me everything that is relevant to this case?" Daniel asked of Grace Petrie. "You have held nothing back, details that would prejudice a satisfactory outcome?"

"I have revealed everything," Grace insisted; "I hold no secrets from you, from anyone."

With hundreds of people staring at Grace, Mr Robeson eased a path through the crowd. Flanked by Daniel and Carys, she followed with unsteady tread.

Daniel led Grace upstairs, to the first floor, to the inquest room. The inquest would commence at 10.30 a.m., therefore officials, witnesses, jurymen and newspaper reporters had already gathered to play their part.

Stern faces looked down from the portraits on the walls, to a large oak table placed in the centre of the room. A hat rail ran along the west wall, a rail already crowded with top hats. A large circular clock ticked away, upon a mantelpiece, behind the coroner's chair. Two large windows provided light and fresh air, their blinds furled, while banks of chairs offered seating for the spectators in the public gallery. Compared with a courtroom, the inquest room was small; crowded with people and additional furniture, it offered a claustrophobic air.

A clerk and a legal assessor flanked the coroner, at the head of the table. Daniel, Mr Robeson and Grace sat to the left, opposite the large windows, while Lewis Murdoch and his assistants sat to the right. Male witnesses would stand at the foot of the table to present their evidence while the court allowed female witnesses a simple wooden chair.

The jury, made up of seventeen respectable men, sat behind Daniel. These men, by trade gardeners, saddlers, grooms and shopkeepers, faced the large oak table and the public gallery. Daniel sensed that the coroner anticipated a split verdict hence the large number of jurymen; possibly twelve would speak as one, and that would serve the needs of this inquest.

With the jurymen sworn in, the coroner, Sir Wyndham Trahearne, prepared to address the court. He sat without a wig, a gown or any formal ceremony, to suit the needs of a coroner's court.

Daniel knew Sir Wyndham Trahearne by reputation and deed. Fifty-eight years old, he lived with his wife and four children in a manor house known locally as the Castle. His ancestors had prospered farming extensive tracts of land. However, now Sir Wyndham Trahearne reaped the rich rewards offered through shares in the iron, coal and railway industries. An intelligent man with an interest in mathematics and science, he owned a luxury paddle steamer and patronised the visual arts.

Sir Wyndham cleared his throat then said, "We are here to determine how Mr Charles Pettigrew Petrie swallowed antimony – as an act of suicide, through misadventure, or through murder. It is my duty to ask you to banish from your minds all that you have read or heard prior to this day and to remind you that you must judge how this gentleman met his death only from the evidence placed before you. However, before we proceed, we have a duty to perform in viewing the body, a duty with which I am sorry to trouble you."

At Daniel's side, Grace shuddered and the advocate's knowing look told Mr Robeson to receive her into his care. Meanwhile, after glancing at Carys, who had taken her place in the public gallery, Daniel accompanied the court officials, his fellow advocates and the jurymen to the graveside, making his way through the crowds gathered in the corridor and the lobby of the hotel.

The inquest party rode to the graveside in a convoy of carriages. There, they viewed the remains of Charles Pettigrew Petrie through a glass panel, inserted into his coffin lid, an adjustment made for the occasion.

In the churchyard, the air was sultry, while the

pungent odour of disinfectants oppressed the atmosphere. Charles lay in an oak coffin decorated with ormolu handles. And while the coffin retained its polish and lustre, the same could not be said of the deceased, for his face and teeth displayed every sign of rapid decay; indeed, they were black.

With heads bowed, and in solemn fashion, the inquest party filed past Charles Petrie's decomposing body. Then, overcome by the humidity and Charles' black grin, one of the jurymen, a shopkeeper, fainted. Two of his colleagues dragged him to his feet. However, his pale features and unsteady demeanour told Daniel that he would not take his place on the bench. One down, sixteen to go, Daniel thought with gallows humour.

"And now that we have viewed the remains," Sir Wyndham Trahearne intoned, "we shall return to the Seabank Hotel and commence the inquest."

* * *

Back at the Seabank Hotel, Daniel found Grace Petrie at Mr Robeson's side. He also found the members in the public gallery in restless mood, their tongues filling the air with impatient chatter. An imperious-looking woman had joined them. Indeed, she looked like the Queen herself. That woman was Mary Petrie, Charles' mother, the instigator of this inquest. Daniel estimated Mary Petrie's age at forty-eight, which meant that she had been a teenager when pregnant with Charles.

With everyone seated, the hubbub of conversation died down. Then the clerk rose to his feet and said, "Call Professor Vernon Pennington."

Dressed in a formal frock coat, and with his head held high and back ramrod straight, Professor Pennington made his way to the foot of the large oak table. There he stood, his gaze firm and unrelenting, fixed on the coroner.

The clerk swore in Professor Pennington. The medical man stated his address in St Hilary then, exuding a sombre air, he awaited Daniel's first question.

Daniel stood with his back to the jurymen, with his body turned towards the professor. He adjusted his notes then said, "Professor Pennington, you performed the post mortem on Charles Petrie's body."

"Indeed, sir, I did."

"Could you please state the condition of Mr Petrie's body?"

"The deceased was in general good health. I detected no illness or abnormalities within the vital organs."

"Except for those organs attacked by the

poison," Daniel said.

"Of course," the professor replied with a gentle inclination of his proud head.

"And antimony was the poison used?"

"It was," Professor Pennington said.

"The condition of Charles Petrie's corpse...is it common for decomposition to set in so quickly after death?"

"In previous cases of antimony poisoning," Professor Pennington said, "though few and far between, the corpses were well preserved. However, those cases involved slow poisoning."

"Therefore," Daniel surmised, "it is safe to say that Charles Petrie ingested one, large dose."

"That is so," Professor Pennington said.

"What quantity of antimony did you discover in Charles Petrie's body?" Daniel asked.

"Twenty grains."

"And that amount would kill a man?"

"I discovered twenty grains," the professor said. "However, I estimate that Charles Petrie consumed forty grains. Forty grains would not only kill a man, that quantity would also kill a horse."

Upon those words, the members in the public galley twittered with nervous laughter. However, a swift glare from the coroner soon restored order.

"And how," Daniel asked, "in your opinion, did Charles Petrie ingest forty grains of antimony?"

"In a solution," the professor said.

"Of water?"

"That is the most likely course. Antimony has no taste when dissolved in water."

Professor Pennington turned to face the coroner. "With the court's permission," he said, "I have prepared a solution of forty grains of antimony in four ounces of water. If they so wish, the learned advocates and jurymen may taste the water to determine that they cannot discern the antimony. However, I strongly advise the gentlemen not to swallow the water."

"With that precaution in mind," Sir Wyndham Trahearne said, "the court grants its permission."

Professor Pennington inclined his head. He summoned an assistant, a young man who entered the courtroom bearing a silver tray laden with a crystal water jug and six crystal glasses. The assistant placed the tray before Professor Pennington then retreated from the room. Meanwhile, the congregation in the public gallery buzzed with anticipation and excitement.

With a steady hand, Professor Pennington poured the antimony-tainted water into the glasses. He offered the glasses to the jurymen, and four of them accepted. He offered a glass to Lewis Murdoch, Mary Petrie's advocate. However, Murdoch turned away, shook his head and declined. Then Professor Pennington offered the final glass to Daniel, who accepted. As Daniel raised the glass to his lips, he glanced at Carys, in the public gallery. She was leaning forward, her left hand gripping her parasol tight, displaying knuckles of white, while her right hand waved a fan in front of her face in furious fashion. Daniel offered Carys a reassuring smile. Then he placed the crystal glass to his lips.

After swilling the water and antimony around in his mouth, Daniel discharged the contents into the finely cut crystal. Then he turned to the jurymen and said, "There is no taste, gentlemen; do you concur?"

Four jurymen nodded as one. They said, "Yes, sir; we concur."

Daniel nodded in turn. Then he sat at the large oak table. Meanwhile, in the public gallery, Carys sighed with relief.

"Thank you, Professor Pennington," Daniel said as Lewis Murdoch rose to his feet.

Dressed in his baggy trousers, long morning coat and double-breasted waistcoat, Lewis Murdoch smiled at Professor Pennington. He fingered the bristles of his heavy, unkempt moustache. Then he adjusted the monocle over his right eye. Despite his dishevelled appearance, Lewis Murdoch was a performer in court, a Henry Irving of the legal profession.

With a flamboyant wave of his right hand, he said to Professor Pennington, "You were called to Charles Petrie's bedside."

"Indeed, sir, I was."

"On the second afternoon of his illness."

"That is true, sir, as well."

"How did you find the patient?"

"In a state of extreme distress."

"And how did you find his wife?" Murdoch asked, his gaze now fixed on Grace.

"In a state of nervous agitation," Professor Pennington said.

"Did she offer up an explanation; did she elucidate as to why she had delayed in calling you? After all, Professor Pennington, you are the most qualified doctor in the county to deal with a case of acute poisoning."

The professor's lips twitched into a thin smile upon receiving the compliment. However, in a stern voice he said, "I assumed that, initially, she did not suspect poisoning."

Lewis Murdoch inclined his head. He adjusted his monocle then said, "Could you please explain, in detail, how the antimony killed Charles Petrie?"

Professor Pennington cleared his throat. He said, "It is remarkable that we have only recorded a small number of fatal antimony cases. This is because antimony's violent emetic action prevents the destroying of life; after consumption, the stomach soon ejects the poison. The sooner the stomach throws off the poison the less likely it is to be absorbed into the blood. Charles Petrie was killed, not by the local irritant action on his stomach, but by the absorption of the poison into his system where it produced fatal results. Unquestionably, during those early hours of unconsciousness, his circulation was absorbing the poison and it was that absorption that killed him."

"At the first inquest," Lewis Murdoch said, "you suggested that Charles Petrie committed suicide."

Professor Pennington inclined his head. He said, "That was my considered opinion."

"Yet," Lewis Murdoch said, "I am sure you would agree antimony is not a drug associated with suicide."

"I agree," the professor said, "it is not."

"How many cases of suicide by antimony have you dealt with?"

"None," Professor Pennington said.

Lewis Murdoch smiled. He glanced at the jurymen. Then he turned his gimlet eyes towards Professor Pennington. "The jury at the previous inquest returned an open verdict, thus casting doubt upon your theory of suicide. Rather eloquently, you have just demonstrated that Charles Petrie could have consumed the antimony without being aware of the fact. Surely this proves that the jurymen in the first inquest were right to find cause for suspicion?"

Before the professor could answer, Murdoch continued, "Let me rephrase the question – in cases of poisoning, surely suspicion is at the forefront of one's mind?"

Professor Pennington pursed his lips. He offered a slow inclination of his head then said, "Your words contain a certain truth."

Lewis Murdoch pirouetted to face the jury. He said, "And I am certain that this inquest will determine the one relevant fact – the truth is murder, not suicide."

As Murdoch returned to his chair, Daniel climbed to his feet. Addressing the professor, he said, "One further question, sir. If you had tended Charles Petrie within the first hour, could you have saved him?"

Professor Pennington paused. He considered the question, then said, "The proper antidote to antimony is a vegetable astringent, which would render the poison insoluble and therefore less active. An antidote applied immediately might have saved Charles Petrie's life. However, I would remind you that he had consumed a large dose, a dose large enough to claim a life."

Daniel inclined his head. He said, "Thank you again, Professor Pennington."

\* \* \*

"Call Florrie Williams," the clerk said, and the maid made her way to the foot of the large oak table. She had dressed for the occasion, Daniel noted, donning a simple lace bonnet, a smart woollen shawl and a pair of long pendant earrings, which dangled prettily from her petite ears. The earrings were special to Florrie, Daniel guessed, and she wore them as badges of honour, in defiance of her servant status.

After the legal preliminaries, Lewis Murdoch rose to his feet and said, "You are Florrie Williams, Grace Petrie's housemaid."

"That is correct, sir."

"And your address?"

"The Grange, sir, at Sker."

"You tended Charles Petrie on the night of his illness."

"I did, sir, with Mrs Quinn's help."

"And what of Grace Petrie at this time?"

"She was asleep, sir, in her bed."

Lewis Murdoch opened his eyes wide; he allowed his monocle to fall against the tweed of his waistcoat in a display of mock astonishment. "Grace Petrie's husband lay dying, and still the woman slept?"

"My mistress was in recovery from a miscarriage, sir. That day was her first day out after her confinement. She was very tired come evening. And..."

"And?" Lewis Murdoch leaned forward. He placed the monocle to his right eye and stared at Florrie Williams. "Would you care to elaborate, miss?"

Florrie swallowed hard. She licked her dry lips. "And," she said, faltering over her words, "my mistress had drunk a lot of sherry, sir."

"How much sherry?" Lewis Murdoch asked.

"A full bottle, sir."

"Is Mrs Petrie in the habit of consuming so much sherry?"

Florrie glanced at Grace Petrie. Then she turned away and bit her bottom lip. "I would rather not say, sir."

"You have no choice in the matter, my dear; you must answer the question. And, I would remind you, you are under oath; you must answer with truth and candour."

Once again, Florrie glanced at Grace. Once again, she swallowed hard and licked her dry lips. "Yes, sir," Florrie said, "my mistress drinks a lot of sherry; she consumes a bottle a day."

With all eyes on Grace, sniggers and laughter emanated from the onlookers in the public gallery. However, in a firm, calm voice, Sir Wyndham Trahearne called for order. Then he said, "Proceed, Mr Murdoch."

"And besides the sherry," Lewis Murdoch said, "does Mrs Petrie consume other beverages?"

"A glass of Marsala at breakfast, sir, and at bedtime. And sometimes a glass or two of brandy and burgundy. And champagne. And a selection of other fine wines."

Cries of 'shame' and 'disgraceful' mingled with laughter as the onlookers in the public gallery mocked Grace. Meanwhile, Florrie looked away, her teeth chewing on her bottom lip, while at Daniel's side, and close to tears, Grace lowered her head in embarrassment.

"Order! Order!" Sir Wyndham Trahearne cried, his right wrist flicking a gavel against a wooden block. As calm descended, he turned to Daniel and said, "Your witness, Mr Morgan."

Daniel stood. He turned to the maid and smiled. "Is this your first inquest, Florrie?"

"It is, sir."

"The atmosphere must feel quite intimidating."

"It does, sir."

"Would you like a drink of water?" Daniel

asked. He reached for an elegant carafe and a fine crystal glass. Then he smiled broadly as he recalled Professor Pennington's earlier demonstration with the antimony and his carafe. "I promise you, Florrie, this water does not contain poison."

Daniel poured a measure of water into a glass. He took a sip. Reassured, Florrie accepted a second glass.

"Thank you, sir," she said.

After Florrie had quenched her thirst and moistened her lips, Daniel asked, "When you woke your mistress, what was her reaction?"

"Confusion, sir. Shock."

"She was upset?"

"Yes, sir; she was tearful. I had to fetch several items of lace to dry her eyes."

"During this time, did Charles Petrie say anything to you?"

"On the first night of his illness, he was in a great deal of pain. He mumbled some words. But he spoke mainly to the doctors, to Mrs Petrie and Mrs Quinn."

"On the second day," Daniel said, "I understand that Mr Petrie enjoyed a short period of relief."

"Yes, sir; he drank some milk, and a glass of champagne."

"And after those drinks?"

"The master was sick, sir. He said to me, he was sorry for being such a burden."

"You cleaned Charles Petrie's face and bed after he was sick?"

"I did, sir."

"Under the doctors' instructions?"

"Yes, sir."

"By the second afternoon," Daniel asked, "do you think that Mr Petrie had accepted his fate?"

Florrie inclined her head. In a small voice she said, "I believe he had, sir."

Daniel paused. He glanced at the jurymen, and at the men and women in the public gallery. He had captured their attention; apart from the occasional cough and the shuffling of feet on the highly polished floorboards, all remained silent.

With his mind firmly upon the maid, Daniel asked, "At any time during his confinement, did Mr Petrie have harsh words to say to his wife, or about his wife?"

"Not one, sir."

Daniel nodded. He said, "Thank you, Florrie."

In turn, the maid offered a shy smile. She said, "Thank you, sir."

* * *

The clerk said, "Call Mrs Quinn."

124

Dressed in a black hat decorated with a dark rose at its centre and feathers at its side, Grace Petrie's former confidant entered the makeshift courtroom. She also wore a long, flowing skirt and a matching black shawl while, in her left hand, she carried a silver-tipped cane. With deliberation and great care, she set the cane to one side as she took her seat at the foot of the large oak table.

After the clerk had sworn in Mrs Jennet Quinn and she had stated her address, Daniel said, "You tended Charles Petrie at the onset of his illness."

The woman in black adjusted her wire-framed spectacles. She replied in a painfully quiet voice, "I did."

"Mrs Quinn," the coroner intervened, "would you kindly speak up; the jurymen cannot hear you."

"I tended Charles Petrie," Mrs Quinn said, her voice no louder, still barely audible.

Daniel glanced at Sir Wyndham Trahearne. However, the coroner merely shrugged, for what more could he do?

"In your own words," Daniel said, "please describe Charles Petrie's condition."

"He was weak," Mrs Quinn said. "I helped him to the window, where he was sick. Then, with Florrie's help, I placed him on the bed."

"In his lucid moments, did he say anything to you?"

"He said, 'I have taken poison.'"

At this revelation, the men and women in the public gallery gasped, all except Mary, Charles Petrie's mother. With her features impassive, apparently set in stone, she stared at Daniel.

"Those were his exact words?" Daniel asked Mrs Quinn.

"His exact words were, 'I have taken poison, don't tell Grace.'"

"Why did Charles say, 'don't tell Grace?'"

Mrs Quinn stared at a knot in the old oak table. Her gloved fingers circled that knot in slow deliberate fashion. She looked up and whispered, "To save her from any further pain, I imagine."

"Did Charles name the poison?"

"He did not."

"How did Charles take the poison?"

"He did not say."

Daniel paused. Everyone in the courtroom was leaning forward; indeed, many had placed a hand behind an ear, to catch Mrs Quinn's words.

Addressing the woman in black, Daniel said, "After Charles Petrie had vomited, you ordered Florrie to clean his bedroom."

"I did."

"Why?"

"To make it presentable to the doctors."

"And what of the evidence?" Daniel asked.

Once again, Mrs Quinn stared at the old oak table, at her gloved index finger as it scribed yet another small, deliberate circle. She whispered, "At that stage, I was unaware of the seriousness of Mr Petrie's condition."

"But a sample of the vomit was gathered?"

"Yes," Mrs Quinn said, "from the leads outside the bedroom window, on the instruction of Professor Pennington."

"And what of Grace Petrie's reaction to her husband's condition?"

Mrs Quinn glanced towards Grace. The woman in black caught her eye then, abruptly, both women turned away. "Grace was upset," Mrs Quinn said.

"I understand," Daniel said, "that at one point Grace fell asleep with her arms around her husband."

"She did," Mrs Quinn confirmed.

"Surely that sounds like the action of a loving wife?"

"It does," she agreed.

Daniel sat on his wooden chair. Meanwhile, Sir Wyndham Trahearne said, "Your witness, Mr Murdoch."

With a flourish, Lewis Murdoch climbed to his feet. He adjusted his monocle, fingered his unruly moustache then said, "Please tell me, Mrs Quinn, how you and Mr Petrie addressed each other."

"We were on first-name terms."

"You called him Charles and he called you Jennet?"

"That is correct."

"Therefore," Lewis Murdoch said, "your relationship went beyond the realms of master and servant."

"I believe we were friends," Mrs Quinn said, "of a kind." She adjusted her bonnet, smoothed the silver streaks in her ebony hair then added with a shy smile, "I trust that you understand me."

Lewis Murdoch inclined his head. He fiddled with his monocle. Then he proceeded to clean its glass upon a crumpled handkerchief. With his handkerchief in his trouser pocket and his monocle firmly in place, he said, "Mrs Petrie called six doctors to tend her husband."

"She did."

"But what of Dr Collymore, her one-time physician?"

"She did not call him," Mrs Quinn said.

"Why did she not call him?"

"I do not know," Mrs Quinn said.

"I would remind you, Mrs Quinn, that you are under oath," Lewis Murdoch said, his tone heavy, burdened with authority, his gaze censorious.

Mrs Quinn placed a gloved hand to her lips, to stifle a polite cough. Suitably composed, she said,

"Charles did not trust Dr Collymore; the doctor was barred from the Grange."

"Did Grace Petrie have any contact with Dr Collymore over those fateful three days?"

Mrs Quinn inclined her head. She said, "Grace asked me to send word to him."

"Which you did."

"Which I did," Mrs Quinn said.

Lewis Murdoch nodded. He smiled. Then he pirouetted to face the jury. "So," he reasoned, "Grace Petrie instructed you to send word to Dr Collymore, a man barred from the Grange. And she did so in the knowledge that if Mr Petrie had learned about her actions it would surely have aggravated his condition."

"Yes," Mrs Quinn said.

A low murmur rippled around the courtroom. Three of the jurors reached for their pens and scribbled notes in their notebooks. Meanwhile, Lewis Murdoch smiled through his moustache. Turning to Jennet Quinn, he asked, "What did Dr Collymore recommend?"

"He recommended cold water applications to the stomach, a mustard plaster on the spine and doses of arsenicum."

Murdoch asked, "Did you apply Dr Collymore's recommendations?"

"The doctors forbade the use of the cold water

and the mustard plaster on the grounds that they would only have increased Charles' pain. However, they allowed Grace to administer small doses of arsenicum."

"Did the arsenicum offer Charles Petrie any relief?" Murdoch asked.

"It did not," Mrs Quinn said.

"Therefore," he reasoned, "Dr Collymore's intervention was in vain."

Jennet Quinn lowered her head. She sighed then said, "Yes, sir; his intervention was in vain."

* * *

Late in the afternoon, Lewis Murdoch called Dr James Onesiphorus Collymore. The clerk swore in Dr Collymore and the physician stated his address. Dressed in a top hat, which he removed, grey serge trousers, a high-collared white shirt, a small black tie and a large frock coat, the revered gentleman took his position at the foot of the witness table.

However, before Lewis Murdoch could begin his questioning, Daniel rose to his feet.

Addressing Sir Wyndham Trahearne, Daniel said, "I know it is custom for male witnesses to stand and for female witnesses to sit when presenting their evidence, but given this gentleman's advanced years, may I suggest that the court offers him a seat."

Sir Wyndham narrowed his eyes, frowned and gazed at Lewis Murdoch. "Do you have any objections, Mr Murdoch?"

In turn, Murdoch waved a casual, dismissive hand and said, "No, Mr Coroner; I have no objections."

Dr Collymore adjusted his pince-nez. He smiled at Daniel, straightened his frock coat then sat at the witness table.

After pausing for dramatic effect, and to ensure that the jurymen were staring at him, Lewis Murdoch said to Dr Collymore, "You knew Grace Petrie and her family from when she was a child."

Dr Collymore inclined his head. In a firm voice, he said, "That is correct."

"You tended Grace Petrie during her marriage to Captain Gustav Trelawney."

"That is correct."

Murdoch paused. He removed his monocle then, in quizzical fashion, he arched his right eyebrow. "For what reason?" he asked.

"She was in a state of nervous distress."

"What brought on this debilitating state?"

"Sadly, Captain Gustav Trelawney beat her while under the influence of alcohol."

At Daniel's side, Grace shuddered at the memory. She sighed and lowered her head.

"And your treatment?" Murdoch asked of Dr Collymore.

"Spa baths, wet-packings and spinal washes; the full range of my hydropathic treatments."

"Was Grace Petrie, Grace Trelawney as was, pleased with the outcome?"

"I believe so," Dr Collymore said.

"After her treatment," Murdoch continued, "Grace Petrie held you in the highest esteem, as a doctor."

"I believe she did."

"Therefore," Murdoch scowled, screwing his monocle firmly in place, "why did she not contact you the moment her husband was taken ill?"

Dr Collymore adjusted his neat tie. He fingered his top hat, which sat beside him, on the table. "Maybe," he ventured, "Mrs Petrie thought that my presence at the Grange would have added to Mr Petrie's distress."

"The man was dying," Murdoch scoffed, "yet your presence at the Grange would have added to his distress; how so?"

"Maybe he didn't hold me in the highest regard."

"Did you ever talk with Charles Petrie?"

"I never met the gentleman," Dr Collymore said.

"Then why should the man hold you in such

low esteem?"

Dr Collymore stared at his top hat. Meanwhile, the sun streamed in through the window, highlighting the hat, casting a long shadow. As the ladies in the public gallery waited for Dr Collymore to answer, they fanned themselves with delicate fans, many trimmed with fine lace.

Eventually, Dr Collymore said, "I can only surmise that Mr Petrie had no respect for my methods."

"But your methods are renowned," Lewis Murdoch said; he waved his right arm, as though to heighten the drama; "you have a fine reputation."

"Amongst my peers," Dr Collymore conceded, "yes."

"Do you use antimony in your hydrotherapies?" Murdoch asked, leaning forward, glaring at Dr Collymore.

"Very rarely," the physician said.

"But you are aware of its properties."

"I am."

"You know full well that antimony can kill a man."

"It is a poison," Dr Collymore said. "Everyone knows that antimony can kill a man."

Murdoch paused. Through his glinting monocle, he stared at the jurymen. As one, they gazed at Dr Collymore. Indeed, within the silent courtroom, all eyes were upon the doctor.

Breaking the silence, Murdoch asked, "Who murdered Charles Petrie?"

Leaping to his feet, Daniel said, "I must object, Mr Coroner. The jurymen are sitting to establish whether or not a murder took place; Mr Murdoch is being disingenuous with his question."

The coroner, Sir Wyndham Trahearne, offered a tired nod of his head. He said, "Kindly rephrase your question, Mr Murdoch."

Lewis Murdoch smiled. He bowed towards Sir Wyndham. "My pleasure, Mr Coroner." Then, with his gaze upon Dr Collymore, he asked, "How did Charles Petrie meet his end?"

"I was not present," Dr Collymore said; "I can only speculate."

"You are a learned man," Murdoch said, "please speculate."

Avoiding the challenge, Dr Collymore said, "I understand that he possessed a deep knowledge of medicines."

"And from whom did you glean that information?"

"Mrs Quinn."

All eyes turned to stare at Mrs Quinn, who sat in the far corner of the courtroom, her gloved fingers inscribing small circles upon the head of her silver-tipped cane.

"You are familiar with Mrs Quinn," Lewis Murdoch said.

"We have met, on occasion."

"And Charles Petrie's demise," Murdoch said, returning to his original question, "would you be kind enough to share your thoughts?"

Dr Collymore paused. He steepled his fingers and angled them towards the jury. It was a submissive gesture, Daniel reflected, as though, subconsciously, he was pleading with the jury for their forgiveness. To Lewis Murdoch, Dr Collymore said, "I believe Professor Pennington suggested suicide."

"Do you concur with Professor Pennington?"

Dr Collymore inclined his head. He said, "I see no reason to contradict him."

"However," Lewis Murdoch said, "the jury at the first inquest established the fact that Charles Petrie was a man of good disposition and not of a melancholy nature. What in this world would move such a man to suicide?"

Dr Collymore averted his gaze. He stared sightlessly at the leaves on the trees as they fluttered outside the window.

A magpie settled on a branch, then flew away. In the distance, a dog barked. In the town, the wooden wheels of a cart creaked as they rolled along a metalled road.

Meanwhile, in a quiet voice, Dr Collymore said, "I cannot answer your question."

"Because," Lewis Murdoch said, his voice rising in triumph, "suicide did not take place; what we have here is murder."

"Mr Coroner," Daniel protested, "the jurymen at the first inquest returned an open verdict; they did not dismiss the notion of suicide. Besides," he continued, "it is for the present jury to decide, and not for Mr Murdoch to announce, a charge of murder."

Sir Wyndham Trahearne acknowledged Daniel's comment with a terse nod of his head. Then he turned to Lewis Murdoch and offered him a weary glare. "Please demonstrate more care with your words, Mr Murdoch."

"I apologise, Mr Coroner. However, allow me to suggest to Dr Collymore that suicide did not take place. I know that as a fact; you, Dr Collymore, know that as a fact; so why do you perpetuate the myth of suicide?"

Dr Collymore frowned. Perspiration formed on the crown of his bald head. He searched for words. However, no sound passed from his lips.

"For what reason," Lewis Murdoch asked; "what is your motive, Dr Collymore? What have you to hide?"

"I have nothing to hide," Dr Collymore said, his

cheeks turning scarlet.

Lewis Murdoch nodded. He smiled. "I am sure that the jurymen will remember those words and recall them upon a later day."

## August 15th 1876

The following morning, the interested parties gathered for day two of the inquest into the poisoning of Charles Petrie. Daniel arrived early, at ten o'clock, thirty minutes before the scheduled start. He found Sir Wyndham Trahearne sitting at the large oak table, organising his papers. As the coroner licked a finger and turned a page, Daniel studied the man.

Of medium build and average height, Sir Wyndham Trahearne possessed clear blue eyes, wavy grey hair and a large nose, which sat above a full, neatly trimmed moustache. He wore a morning coat over his waistcoat and pinstriped trousers. A handkerchief protruded from the breast pocket of his morning coat, while a gold watch on a gold chain adorned his waistcoat. Furthermore, a high starched collar sat snug against his proud neck.

Daniel knew Sir Wyndham as a fair man. However, the need for a second inquest had undermined his authority; during the first inquest, he had led the jury towards a verdict of suicide. However, they had failed to agree. Although weakened, as County Coroner, he had a duty to chair the second inquest. On the first day, he had allowed Lewis Murdoch to ride roughshod over legal procedure, and Daniel feared more of the same. Indeed, Sir Wyndham Trahearne offered the impression of a man whose thoughts were on his yacht, sailing in the Mediterranean, which did not bode well for Grace.

At the appointed time, Grace duly arrived, along with Carys Beaumond and Mr Robeson. The trio had forced their way through an even larger crowd and now, inside the courtroom, they sat in their appointed places. Daniel turned to Grace and bid her good morning. She replied with the stench of sherry upon her breath.

While the ladies in the public gallery lowered their parasols and reached for their fans, the clerk read the witness statements from the previous day. Indeed, this procedure would continue upon every day. Duly satisfied, Professor Pennington, Florrie Williams, Jennet Quinn and Dr Collymore signed their statements. Then Daniel called Bert Kemp, the groom, as the first witness of the day.

Kemp arrived in a three-piece suit, which comprised a long lounging jacket, a matching waistcoat and corresponding trousers. He also wore a four-in-the-hand tie and a carnation in his buttonhole. Both the suit and the carnation had seen fresher days.

When the clerk had sworn in Burt Kemp, Daniel said, "I understand, Mr Kemp, that you are a family man."

"Indeed, I am," Kemp replied with a measure of pride. "I have a wife and five children."

"And what of your hobbies?"

"I like a mug of ale and a game of bando."

Daniel paused to study his notes, although in truth he had already filed the facts securely away in his head. Nevertheless, he read a paragraph then said, "You served as a groom for Grace Petrie."

"I did."

"And before that, for Dr Collymore."

"I did."

"On the eve of Charles and Grace Petrie's wedding, you stated that Charles would not live beyond four months into the marriage."

"I did."

"Harsh words," Daniel said.

"They were," Kemp agreed.

"Heartfelt words?"

"They were," Kemp said.

"Why so?"

"Because Mr Petrie had dismissed me and banished me from my home."

"You were angry with Charles Petrie?"

Kemp nodded in vigorous fashion. He glowered. "How would you have felt in my position?"

"Do you use antimony in your work?" Daniel asked.

"I use it to tend sores on the horses and to treat them for worms."

Daniel paused. He flicked through his notes until he located a soiled sheet of paper. "This letter," he said, holding up the sheet of paper, "was sent to Charles Petrie, a week into his marriage; it contains the accusation that he married Grace for her money; the handwriting is similar to yours, wouldn't you agree, Mr Kemp?" Daniel held up a second sheet of paper. He offered both items to the groom. Then he informed the court, "I present here Bert Kemp's log of purchases whilst in Grace Petrie's employment."

Kemp leaned forward. He studied the letter and the purchase log. With a frown creasing his forehead, he said, "The handwriting is similar, I agree."

"Did you send this letter to Charles Petrie?" Daniel asked.

Kemp rolled his eyes. He stared at the ceiling, as though to admire the ornate plasterwork. However, he said, "My mind's a perfect blank; I cannot remember."

Daniel frowned. He said, "You are speaking under oath, Mr Kemp."

Bert Kemp ran his fingers through his rich mane of black hair. Like a man dancing on hot coals, he shuffled from foot to foot. Then he confessed, "I might have written those words, in a fever of hate."

Daniel gathered the paperwork from Bert Kemp and placed it within his notes. Then he turned to question the groom. "Before your dismissal, did you respect Charles Petrie?"

Kemp pushed out his bottom lip. He thought for a considerable time then said, "We had hot words, occasionally."

"Why," Daniel asked, "for what reason?"

"He was not a man I felt comfortable with."

Again, Daniel asked, "For what reason?"

"He often said one thing, but did another."

"You prefer plain-speaking people."

Kemp nodded. "I do."

"You are a plain speaker."

"I am," Kemp agreed, "and I see nothing wrong in that."

Daniel sat while Lewis Murdoch stood. The latter checked his pocket watch, an old trick, to keep the witness on edge. Satisfied with the time, and with the fact that he had allowed Bert Kemp the opportunity to stew, Murdoch asked, "Did you murder Charles Petrie?"

"After my dismissal," Kemp said, "I had no access to the Grange; how could I have murdered him?"

"Was he murdered?" Murdoch asked.

Kemp nodded in solemn fashion. "It's the talk of the parish."

"And what do the people of the parish say?"

"They say that his wife murdered him."

The gasps from the public gallery would have done justice to Drury Lane or the Gaiety Theatre. Those gasps turned into whispers, which extended to the crowd, gathered in the corridor. Someone said, "What did he say?" And his companion replied, "Grace Petrie murdered her husband."

Aware that Lewis Murdoch had inflicted a bloody wound, nevertheless, Daniel rose to offer words of complaint. "Mr Coroner, gossip and hearsay have no place in a court of law."

Sir Wyndham Trahearne inclined his head. He addressed the jury. "Gentlemen of the jury, please dismiss Mr Kemp's comment."

However, the jurymen, like the crowd in the corridor, and the members in the public gallery, had clearly taken Bert Kemp's statement on board; from this moment on there could be no doubt – Grace Petrie was guilty until proven innocent.

Lewis Murdoch sat with a satisfied smile upon his face. He said, "No further questions, Mr Coroner."

* * *

Daniel Morgan decided to take the initiative – he called Grace Petrie.

Escorted by Mr Robeson, Grace walked to the foot of the large oak table. There, she sat while he raised a carafe and poured her a glass of water. Grace stared at the water. With trembling hands, she lifted a heavy crêpe veil to reveal her pale, pinched features. She placed the veil over a small, lace-trimmed bonnet until it cascaded down her back, covering her tightly bound-up hair. Then she removed her black gloves and adjusted her black fichu until it sat snug around her shoulders.

The clerk approached with the Bible, which Grace kissed. Suitably sworn in, she took a deep breath, to aid her composure. Then she turned to face Daniel.

With compassion, the advocate said, "I understand that you have been unwell recently."

"I have," Grace said. She took another deep breath. Then she stared at her right hand and a large emerald ring, which adorned her ring finger. Daniel noted that the ring was a splendid gem and her only item of jewellery.

"You suffered a miscarriage."

Grace inclined her head. She said, "Sadly, I did."

"That was your second miscarriage in three months."

Grace swallowed. Then, while fighting back her tears, she said, "That statement is true."

"I am sure that this court extends its sympathies to you," Daniel said, his words echoed by the members in the public gallery who offered a low murmur of assent.

"In regard to your husband's infirmity," Daniel said, "could you please tell this inquest what happened on the night he was taken ill?"

Grace shuddered at the memory. She reached for her glass and took a sip of water. "I was asleep in my bed," she said. "I felt exhausted. That was the first day in town since my second miscarriage. We had supper, a glass of Marsala...I fell asleep as soon as my head touched the pillow. I woke in a daze when Florrie called me. She said Charles was ill, so I rushed to his room. I found him lying on the bed in great distress."

"What happened then?" Daniel probed.

"I asked him what was the matter, but he couldn't answer. He spoke, but his words were incoherent. So I instructed Florrie to send for Dr Marsh."

"Dr Spofforth had already been summoned."

"Yes," Grace said, "by Mrs Quinn."

"When the doctors arrived, what happened then?"

"They tried to talk with Charles, but he was so ill, troubled with bouts of sickness, he couldn't answer. Eventually, I lay beside him, hugged him, kissed him and fell asleep."

"You were exhausted from your day."

Grace closed her eyes only to open them as though startled. When she spoke, she spoke calmly; however, her trembling hands revealed her troubled nerves. She sighed, "I have felt exhausted for many days."

"How do you account for that?" Daniel asked.

"My miscarriages."

"Have you suffered from other symptoms, apart from the exhaustion?"

"Back pain," Grace said. "And nausea."

"Have any members of staff complained of illness?"

"No," Grace said; "everyone has been in good health."

Daniel thanked Grace. Then he returned to his seat.

Meanwhile, Lewis Murdoch removed a handkerchief from his trouser pocket and mopped a bead of perspiration from his brow. In the public gallery, the men suffered in silence, encased in their heavy woollen suits, while the ladies deployed fans, which fluttered like birds on the wing.

Suitably refreshed, Murdoch stuffed his handkerchief into his trouser pocket. He smiled at Grace. "Do you take any medicines for your symptoms?" he asked, his tone light, shrouded in sincerity.

"I take homeopathic medicines," Grace said, "formerly supplied by Mrs Quinn. And prescription medicines."

"Supplied by Dr Collymore?"

"Initially, yes, but no longer."

"But no longer?" Murdoch opened his eyes wide and his monocle fell from his right eye only to land upon his waistcoat.

"Charles insisted that he should oversee all aspects of the home and my health," Grace explained.

"Therefore," Murdoch surmised, "you did not summon Dr Collymore to tend you because such a summons would have displeased your husband?"

"That is true."

"Why would Dr Collymore's presence at the Grange have displeased your husband?"

"Because Charles disapproved of his methods."

"Your husband did not regard Dr Collymore as a serious doctor?"

"That is true."

"And now that your husband is no longer with us," Murdoch asked, "will you summon Dr Collymore?"

"I will not."

"Why not?" he frowned.

"Because to summon Dr Collymore would be

discourteous to Charles' memory."

Murdoch nodded, as though satisfied. He breathed on his monocle. Then he polished the glass upon his lapel. Content with the glass, he placed it over his right eye. "Did you love your husband?" he asked.

"I felt a great deal of affection for him."

"But not love?"

"What is love?" Grace asked, her tone wistful.

"I am an advocate," Lewis Murdoch said, "not a poet; I cannot say."

The jurymen laughed, along with members of the public gallery. Indeed, even Sir Wyndham Trahearne raised a smile.

"Did you argue with your husband?" Murdoch asked.

Grace reached for her glass, then thought better of it. Instead, she licked her lips and said, "We shared the occasional cross word."

"Over what subject?"

"Money."

"Would you please elaborate," Lewis Murdoch said; "kindly explain to the court."

"I invoked the Married Woman's Property Act and Charles objected."

"By invoking the Act," Murdoch said, "you kept your money and possessions in your own name."

"That is true."

"With all candour," Murdoch smiled, "your conduct was not becoming of a loyal and loving wife."

"It seemed the prudent thing to do," Grace said, her eyes lowered, her voice small, "at the time."

"Did you not trust your husband?"

"I did not truly know him."

"Yet," Murdoch scoffed, "you married him. Why did you marry him?"

Grace closed her eyes. She swooned, as though overcome by the moment. Scenting blood, Lewis Murdoch moved in for the kill.

"May I make a suggestion?" he asked. "You married Charles Petrie because you sought respectability. After four years of loneliness, after four years of being shunned by polite society because of your troubled past, you sought a route back into that society. And Charles offered you a route. Am I right, Mrs Petrie?"

With her eyes closed and her hands shaking, Grace reached for her glass of water.

"However," Murdoch continued, "upon marriage, you discovered that you were not compatible. A second divorce would have curtailed all hopes of returning to polite society; therefore, you sought the only option left open to you."

Distressed, Grace knocked over her glass. However, Mr Robeson anticipated the moment and, in one lithe movement, he swooped to retrieve the glass before it could smash upon the floor.

Meanwhile, Daniel leapt to his feet to complain. He said, "I must object, Mr Coroner. Mr Murdoch has stepped way beyond the bounds of decency with his choice of words and thinly veiled accusations."

Sir Wyndham Trahearne inclined his head. With his gavel in his right hand, he said, "Please question the witness, Mr Murdoch; do not speculate."

Murdoch bowed graciously. "But of course, Mr Coroner." Turning to Grace, he said, "I notice that your hair contains a number of blonde flecks...do you use hair dye, Mrs Petrie?"

"Occasionally," Grace said, "yes."

Mr Robeson's intervention had broken her trance and although she spoke with the advocate, her eyes were now on the powerful Nevisian.

Murdoch smiled at Grace. He nodded then said, "I believe that hair dye contains antimony."

Shaking his head in frustration, Daniel climbed to his feet. "Mr Coroner," he said, "once again, I must object. It is common knowledge that the amount of antimony used in hair dye is miniscule. Mr Murdoch makes these comments to cast aspersions upon my client's character and to plant seeds of suspicion in the jurymen's minds."

Indeed, the jurymen were staring at Grace, their expressions grim. The note takers amongst them scribbled notes while the remainder, perspiring to a man, waved their hands in front of their faces to shoo away a troublesome fly.

In turn, Lewis Murdoch glanced at Daniel, at Grace, at the jurymen with a measure of satisfaction. Before Sir Wyndham Trahearne could intervene, he said, "No further questions, Mr Coroner."

\* \* \*

Distressed, Grace Petrie returned to the Grange to take solace in her sherry. Meanwhile, Daniel, eager for exercise, walked with Mr Robeson through the sand dunes. As they walked, Mr Robeson gazed out to sea.

"Do you long to ride the ocean wave again?" Daniel asked, his tone playful.

Mr Robeson smiled. He said, "What you really ask is, do I long to climb the rigging in a force ten gale as we round the Horn, or would I prefer to dine with elegant ladies and civil company?"

"I could supply but only one answer," Daniel said.

Mr Robeson laughed. "And so could I, my

friend, and so could I."

In friendly fashion, Daniel tapped Mr Robeson upon his back. They walked on. Then Daniel asked, "But what of your family and homeland?"

"My sister keeps me well informed," Mr Robeson said. He reached into his velvet waistcoat and extracted a letter. He offered the letter to Daniel. "She has taken up a position as teacher in the local school. She is well. My family are well. With my sister's letters, I retain a link with home."

Daniel returned the letter to Mr Robeson. Then he glanced over his shoulder to spy Carys, who was walking through the sand dunes. In turn, she noticed Daniel and quickened her pace.

"I think it's time I wrote to my sister," Mr Robeson smiled.

The Nevisian acknowledged Carys with a gracious bow. Then he returned to the Prince of Wales Inn.

"You were not at your lodgings," Carys said. "Therefore, I walked the dunes in search of you."

"After a day spent in the stuffy courtroom," Daniel explained, "I felt in need of fresh air."

Carys smiled. Content with his answer, she twirled her parasol in playful fashion.

With the sun sinking in the west, offering a pink glow to the sea and sky, Carys lowered her parasol. She admired the view then turned to face

Daniel. "How did you meet Mr Robeson?" she asked.

"I was in a tavern in Tiger Bay," Daniel explained, "looking for a sailor, in connection with a legal matter. I found the sailor and talked with him. However, as I left the tavern, three thugs set upon me with an eye for my purse. They were about to rob me when Mr Robeson stepped forward and challenged them."

"There was a fight?" Carys frowned.

"A brief skirmish," Daniel explained.

"What happened?" Carys asked, her mouth agape.

Daniel smiled. He said, "Let us just say, the three men discovered that the harbour in winter can be a very cold place."

"And from that moment, you and Mr Robeson became friends?"

"I bought him a drink. We talked into the evening. At nightfall, I offered him a place of employment, which he graciously accepted."

"And the small scar upon your left cheek," Carys asked, "was that inflicted by the robbers?"

Daniel caressed the scar in absent-minded fashion. "No," he said, "I obtained this scar during a swordfight, ostensibly a playful encounter. However, my opponent displayed a pirate's lust for violence, for which he later apologized."

"But you defeated him," Carys said, her tone earnest, supportive, "in the swordfight."

Daniel laughed. "Let us just say that honour was satisfied. And we both walked away, to skirmish another day."

Daniel and Carys walked through the sand dunes until they reached the large freshwater pool. Within and around the pool, Daniel noted the reed beds, the willow trees and a boathouse, built from stone. While gazing at the boathouse, he asked, "Why is Dr Collymore no longer welcome at the Grange?"

Carys paused. She thought for a moment, then said, "Charles was very controlling; he wanted to run his house his way."

"But," Daniel said, "the Grange belongs to Grace; she invoked the Married Woman's Property Act."

"She did," Carys agreed. "And I believe that by invoking the Act it caused bitterness between them, that and his mother interfering."

"Charles' mother interfered in the marriage?"

"It is not for me to speak out of turn," Carys said, "but I believe that his mother stood against the marriage and would have objected to any bride, no matter how pretty, no matter how wealthy."

"Charles belonged to his mother and she would have it no other way?"

Carys inclined her head. Through her natural disposition, she offered Daniel a demure smile. "That was my impression, yes."

Daniel frowned. He caressed his chin. Then his gaze wandered to the clear water of the pool. With a smile, he turned to Carys and asked, "Do you mind if I swim? My muscles are stiff after the court session today."

Carys blushed. For a reason she did not fully understand, she opened her parasol. While twirling the parasol, she said, "If it will ease your muscles, then you should. However, remain mindful of the reeds; they can be dangerous."

Daniel nodded. He removed his velvet jacket and unbuttoned his silk shirt. Placing her parasol over her left shoulder, Carys turned her back on Daniel. She longed for her fan, to cool the heat, which continued to rise on her cheeks.

"You can look now," Daniel said; "I am in the water."

Slowly, Carys turned around. They were alone, she noted, akin to Adam and Eve. Indeed, Daniel was as naked as Adam. With that thought at the forefront of her mind, her cheeks burned scarlet.

"Is the water cold?" Carys asked.

"It is," Daniel said. "However, it soothes my aching muscles." He smiled, "Maybe there is something to be said for Dr Collymore's hydropathic treatments after all."

A strong athlete, Daniel extended his arms and swam towards the centre of the pool. There, he paused. Then he turned to wave at Carys. She waved back, swinging her right arm in enthusiastic fashion.

As Daniel approached dry land, Carys turned her back and raised her parasol. She anticipated his rise from the water, and when that did not occur, she risked a peep, over her shoulder. Daniel was not there; he had disappeared.

Concerned, Carys placed a hand to her breast. While scanning the reeds, she called out, "Mr Morgan! Mr Morgan! Daniel! Daniel! Are you all right?"

Blowing water from his cheeks, Daniel surfaced in front of Carys.

"You gave me a scare," she said, her tone a blend of the censorious and the relieved.

"I am sorry," Daniel said; "that was not my intention." He ran a hand through his wet, dishevelled hair. "I would like to climb out of the water now," he smiled.

Once again, Carys turned her back and raised her parasol. She waited while Daniel dried himself upon his silk shirt. He pulled on his trousers and buttoned his jacket. Then, suitably attired, he walked with Carys, towards the inn.

With his shoes kicking up the sand, Daniel asked, "What are your plans for the future?"

"I shall translate my books and manuscripts," Carys said. "I will marry again and have children."

"First," Daniel mused, "you must find a man of compatible wealth."

Carys paused. She frowned. "Why should I seek a man of compatible wealth? I have riches beyond my requirements; I do not need money; when I marry again, I shall marry for love, be he a simple harpist or a lofty king."

"Then," Daniel said, "that man will be truly blessed."

Daniel waited while a horse and cart rumbled along the road. Then he set foot on the road, his destination the Prince of Wales Inn. However, dumbfounded, Carys remained on the verge, rooted to the spot, with her feet entrenched in the sand.

As Daniel turned to enquire about Carys' welfare, she asked, "Do you really mean that?"

"I do. Come," he said; "you must return to the Hall and I must return to my lodgings; we have a busy day ahead in court tomorrow."

Day three of the inquest into the poisoning of Charles Petrie began when the clerk read aloud the witness statements from the previous day. After the witnesses had signed their statements, Lewis Murdoch called Bert Kemp to offer evidence.

Dressed in his well-worn three-piece suit, clearly his Sunday best, Kemp approached the foot of the witness table. There, he adjusted his buttonhole, which contained a fresh carnation.

Murdoch paused, for dramatic effect, then he launched into his questioning. "Mr Kemp, when you worked for Grace Petrie, did she visit you at the stables?"

"On occasion," Kemp said.

"Why did she visit you?"

"To talk about the horses, Cremorne and Victor."

"And to ride the horses?"

"Not much in recent times," Kemp said.

"Why is that?" Murdoch asked.

"Because Mrs Petrie was not in the best of health."

"Due to her fondness for sherry?"

"I wouldn't know, sir," Kemp said; "I'm not a medical man, I'm not a doctor."

"You are not a doctor," Murdoch agreed.

"However, you are familiar with antimony."

Kemp nodded. He thrust out his chin then said, "I have already admitted as such."

"Did Grace Petrie ever talk with you about antimony?"

"She did."

"What did you discuss?"

"She asked about its properties. She asked what it did for the horses and if it was safe."

"Did she ask about the properties of antimony, regarding people?"

"She did. She asked if I'd accidentally swallowed some and its effects on me."

"Did Grace Petrie ask any other questions about antimony?"

"She asked where one might procure it."

A low murmur swept through the courtroom, followed by the shuffling of feet, the adjusting of clothing and a bout of nervous coughing.

Unperturbed, Lewis Murdoch checked his pocket watch. He polished the watch on the fabric of his waistcoat. Then while looking up he said, "You stated, quite forcefully, that Charles Petrie would not live beyond four months into the marriage."

"I did."

"By that, did you imply that someone," Murdoch paused to glance at Grace, "would poison

Mr Petrie?"

"I did not imply anything of the sort," Kemp said. "I gave no thought to my words. I speak in the moment, as I see fit."

Lewis Murdoch inclined his head. He acknowledged Sir Wyndham Trahearne. Then he resumed his seat at the witness table.

With all eyes upon him, Daniel stood. He glanced at his legal papers, absorbed a note, then said, "Mr Kemp, would you please describe the stables."

"At the Grange?"

"Yes," Daniel said, "at the Grange."

Kemp frowned. He caressed the stubble on his pockmarked chin. "Well," he said, "when I worked at the Grange the establishment contained a four-stall stable, a loose box, a harness room and a carriage house."

"And the establishment also contained shelves and cupboards, for potions and medicines?"

"It did," Kemp agreed.

"Regarding Mrs Petrie's questions about antimony; they could have been the questions of the curious, could they not?"

Kemp pursed his lips. Once again, he scratched his chin. "I suppose they could," he conceded.

"They could have been the questions of someone who cared about her horses and their welfare."

"They could," he agreed.

"Did Grace Petrie take an interest in the other servants at the Grange?"

"She always had a kind word for them, when I was there. She took an interest in the gardener's work, and the gardens in particular."

"Therefore," Daniel said, "Grace Petrie's questions about antimony could have been innocent questions."

Kemp shrugged. He conceded, "I suppose they could."

"Have you ever poisoned a horse with antimony, by accident?" Daniel asked.

Bert Kemp examined his right thumb. That thumb contained an abrasion and the abrasion had worn the sensitive skin on his chin into a sore spot. "I can't recall," he said; "my mind's a perfect blank."

Daniel smiled. He said, "Have you ever troubled a doctor to tend your blank mind, Mr Kemp?"

In an angry outburst, Kemp leaned forward and yelled, "I did not poison Mr Petrie!"

"No one said you did."

Daniel turned and addressed Sir Wyndham Trahearne. In a calm, serene voice, he said, "Thank you, Mr Coroner; no more questions for this witness."

* * *

After a break for mid-morning refreshment, Florrie Williams found herself sitting on the witness chair.

Lewis Murdoch circled Florrie like a vulture circling its prey. "Do you find it a strain," he asked, "tending your mistress?"

"A strain, sir?" Florrie frowned.

"Because she is not in the best of health."

"It is not a strain, sir; I enjoy my work at the Grange."

"But you have nursed your mistress constantly in recent times."

"Through two miscarriages, sir; with Mrs Quinn's help."

"And before the miscarriages," Murdoch asked, "was Grace Petrie in good health?"

"Some days, sir, she was."

"And on other days?"

"She felt giddy."

Raucous laughter erupted from the public gallery. Wearing a censorious frown, Sir Wyndham Trahearne picked up his gavel and demanded silence. Meanwhile, on her seat beside Daniel, Grace lowered her head in despair.

"Why did your mistress feel 'giddy'?" Murdoch

asked, his smile recalling the cat that had licked the cream.

"I wouldn't know, sir," Florrie said, the maid faltering over her words.

"Because of her fondness for sherry?" Murdoch suggested.

"I couldn't say, sir."

Murdoch paused. He placed his right hand over his left and examined his fingernails. His fingernails were pitted and dimpled, which suggested psoriasis of the nails.

Placing his hands in his waistcoat pockets, Murdoch asked, "Apart from her miscarriages and the giddy spells induced by sherry, has Grace Petrie suffered from any serious bouts of illness?"

"I think not, sir," Florrie said, her gaze lowered, her voice soft.

"Think carefully, Florrie," Murdoch coaxed.

"There was one occasion," Florrie said. She looked up. However, she did not dare to meet Grace's gaze.

"What happened on that occasion?" Murdoch asked.

"My mistress lost a lot of blood, sir. Her blood covered the sheets; I washed them for a week before they would come clean."

"What misfortune befell your mistress?" Murdoch asked. "What calamity caused her to lose so much blood?"

"A tumour," Florrie whispered, "the doctor said."

"Which doctor?" Murdoch asked.

Florrie turned towards a bench, which sat in the far corner of the courtroom. The witnesses resided upon that bench, including Dr Collymore.

"Speak up," Murdoch demanded. "Which doctor?"

"Dr Collymore," Florrie said, averting her gaze.

"Did this incident occur before Grace's marriage to Charles Petrie?"

"It did, sir."

"When, exactly, did this misfortune occur?"

"In the first month of my employment, sir; two years and one month before the marriage."

"And Dr Collymore tended Grace Petrie on that occasion?"

"Yes, sir."

"What was the nature of the tumour?" Murdoch asked, his head canted to the right, his facial muscles screwed up tight to hold his monocle in place.

"I couldn't say, sir."

Murdoch smiled. He relaxed his facial muscles and his monocle fell against his waistcoat. However, he paid it no heed. "You are loyal to your mistress."

"And through my loyalty, sir, I speak the truth."

Murdoch inclined his head. He said, "I am sure you do, Florrie; you speak the truth as you see it, or as you are told to recall it."

Florrie bit her bottom lip. She lowered her head in embarrassment. Sensing her distress, Daniel climbed to his feet. "Mr Coroner," he said, "Mr Murdoch casts a slight upon the witness."

Sir Wyndham Trahearne caressed his gavel. He leaned back in his chair. Through tired eyes, he offered Lewis Murdoch a troubled stare. "That comment was uncalled for, Mr Murdoch.

The advocate bowed his head in supplication and offered his apologies. Then, straightening his back, he said, "Clearly, we require a medical opinion; I move that we call Dr Collymore."

\* \* \*

Due to his advanced age, the court allowed Dr Collymore a seat at the witness table. Although dapper and well presented in his serge trousers and high-collared shirt, today the doctor looked ill at ease. Indeed, his complexion was florid while the whites of his eyes, devoid of their pince-nez, revealed an intricate pattern of small red veins, akin to the burgeoning railway network.

Standing, Lewis Murdoch glanced at the jurymen, to ensure that he had captured their full attention. Then he questioned Dr Collymore.

"Tell me, sir; is it true; you removed a tumour from Grace Petrie?

"It is true."

"You performed an operation on Grace Petrie."

"I did."

"Are you qualified to perform such an operation?"

"I am a doctor," Dr Collymore said with some pride.

"But not a surgeon."

Dr Collymore placed a finger between his neck and shirt collar. He adjusted the collar. Then he flexed his neck muscles, a gesture that caused him some pain. "It was an emergency," he said.

Lewis Murdoch compressed his lips. He offered the doctor a look that bordered on the sceptical. "When did this operation take place?"

"Approximately two years ago."

"You performed this operation because it was an emergency?"

"I did."

"And how did you reach that conclusion?"

Dr Collymore loosened his small black tie. He swallowed hard. Then he eased his shirt button away from his neck. "I reached that conclusion through the extreme loss of blood."

Lewis Murdoch inclined his head. He glanced at Grace then said, "Pray tell me, doctor, from which region of Grace Petrie's body did the blood pour?"

The physician shuffled in his seat. He reached for a glass of water. After he had sipped the water, he turned to Sir Wyndham Trahearne and said, "Mr Coroner, I would rather not say."

"From the gynaecological region?" Lewis Murdoch persisted.

"I would rather not say."

"You performed an abortion, did you not, Dr Collymore." Although a short man, Lewis Murdoch stood tall in triumph. "Is that the reason for your reticence?"

"I did not perform an abortion," Dr Collymore insisted.

"I would remind you," Lewis Murdoch said, his tone grave, his features solemn, "you are under oath, Dr Collymore."

Once again, the doctor glanced at Sir Wyndham Trahearne. As he spoke, beads of perspiration formed on the dome of his bald head. With a grimace, he complained, "I object to this line of questioning, Mr Coroner."

"Who fathered Grace Petrie's unborn child?" Lewis Murdoch asked.

"Mr Coroner," Daniel said, climbing to his feet. "I must object; this court is sitting to determine how Charles Petrie consumed poison; it is not sitting in judgement of my client's character."

Sir Wyndham frowned. He stared at his gavel. With his eyes downcast, he asked, "Are these questions relevant, Mr Murdoch?"

"Highly relevant, Mr Coroner." Lewis Murdoch straightened his waistcoat. With a spring in his step, he approached Dr Collymore. "Need I repeat the question?" he asked.

"Grace was ill," Dr Collymore said. "The operation was essential, to save her life."

"You took a life," Lewis Murdoch scowled.

"I saved a life," Dr Collymore insisted. In a rush, he stumbled over his words, "If Grace had have, should have, died, the baby would have died too."

"You took a life," Lewis Murdoch said.

"I performed an operation to save a life."

"Abortions are illegal," Lewis Murdoch reminded the court.

"It was not an abortion," Dr Collymore said; "it was an operation to save a life."

"And what of the father," Lewis Murdoch demanded; "could you offer a name?"

Flustered, Dr Collymore threw his hands into the air. He shook his head and said, "I would not like to speculate."

"Speculate?" Lewis Murdoch scoffed. "You mean to tell us, we are to be offered a choice?"

With that, the public gallery erupted in fits of laughter. A portly man, a butcher, actually held his sides. Daniel noted that many tradesmen had lined the public gallery today. They had forsaken their trades for the day, to enjoy a morning and afternoon of legal sport.

At the witness table, Dr Collymore placed his left hand to his forehead. He said, "I was careless with my words. I meant to say, I do not know of the father."

"However," Lewis Murdoch said, "you can confirm that Grace Petrie, a widow of two years, was with child."

"I can," Dr Collymore said, his voice faint.

Now, the laughter within the courtroom gave way to gasps of astonishment. Many in the public gallery called out, "Shame! Shame! While others hurled insults. Struggling to maintain order, Sir Wyndham bashed his gavel upon its block, while Grace lowered her head, mortified.

"Did Grace Petrie consent to your operation?" Lewis Murdoch asked.

"She did."

"Thus, Grace Petrie consented to the taking of a life."

"I performed an operation," Dr Collymore said, "to save a life."

The centre of attention, Lewis Murdoch walked around the courtroom. He paused beside the window, placed a finger to his chin and adopted a thoughtful pose. Then, as though reciting a soliloquy, he said, "Allow me to clarify the facts in my own mind: Grace Petrie, a widow of two years, a woman who abandoned her first husband, a woman who stood by and allowed her first husband to die, a woman who inherited a large sum of money from her first husband and withheld that money from her second husband, a woman who fell into the arms of an unknown lover, or lovers, consented to the taking of a life. I ask you, sirs, what manner of iniquity is this? What are we to make of Grace Petrie, of her character? What are we to make of the woman who sits before us in this court?"

"Mr Coroner," Daniel said, his voice firm, his demeanour demanding respect, "once again, may I remind you and the jurymen that this court is sitting to determine how Charles Petrie consumed poison; it is not sitting in judgement of my client's character."

Sir Wyndham inclined his head towards Daniel. He puffed out his cheeks and sighed, "Mr Murdoch, you have made your point."

Lewis Murdoch turned to glance at the jury.

However, to a man they were staring at Grace. "I believe I have," he said with a smile.

* * *

With the jurymen's gaze upon her, Grace walked towards the witness seat. There, she adjusted her black crêpe mourning dress and a set of heavy jet jewellery. She had donned the dress and the jewellery to remind the jury that she was in mourning, a widow and, like Charles, a victim.

However, Lewis Murdoch was in no mood for sympathy. Without any preamble, he resumed his attack. "You met Bert Kemp in the stables and talked with him about antimony."

"I asked my questions out of curiosity," Grace said, "not out of malice."

"You had no intention of gaining knowledge of antimony from Bert Kemp to poison your husband?"

Grace's pale cheeks coloured with indignation. She scowled, "That is an outrageous suggestion."

In support of his client, Daniel rose to his feet. "Mr Coroner..."

Sir Wyndham acknowledged Daniel. Then, with a deep frown creasing his forehead, he said, "Kindly rephrase your question, Mr Murdoch."

"Certainly, Mr Coroner," Murdoch said. "Mrs

Petrie, on the night of your abortion, for abortion it surely was, did you summon Dr Collymore specifically?"

"I did," Grace said.

"Even though he is not a gynaecological doctor?"

"He is not a gynaecological doctor," Grace agreed. "However, Dr Collymore had been treating me for my general health."

"By that," Murdoch said, "do you mean that he had been treating you for your fondness for sherry?"

"He had been treating me for my general health," Grace replied through clenched teeth.

From his position at the large oak table, Daniel sensed that Grace had steeled herself for this encounter; she had arrived in a more belligerent mood.

"And what of the child's father," Murdoch asked; "did you summon him?"

Grace glared at Murdoch. However, she did not deign to answer. Meanwhile, the newspaper reporters, who sat at a bench adjacent to the witness table, took in every detail. Some studied the principal players while others scribbled notes. They would transcribe those notes into newspaper copy and those newspapers would inform millions of readers, enlighten them as to Grace's woes.

"I assume," Murdoch said, "that you will not claim Immaculate Conception and thus admit to the fact that you did enter into illegal congress."

"It was an act of love," Grace insisted, "not an illegal act."

"One act," Murdoch smiled, "or several acts?"

Grace blushed. She placed her hands on the witness table and, Daniel noticed, her fingers started to shake. She took a deep breath then said, "I do not see how these questions are relevant to my husband's death."

"You were pregnant," Murdoch said, "out of wedlock, and you do not see the relevance?"

"I gave in to temptation on one occasion," Grace said, raising her voice; "am I forever to be blighted by that night?"

Murdoch paused. He glanced at the newspaper reporters. To a man, they were scribbling now, their notebooks jostling for position amongst a plethora of top hats, removed from their heads and placed on the bench.

Returning to Grace, Lewis Murdoch said, "You recognize that your temptation was a sin?"

"It was an act of love," Grace said.

Murdoch shrugged. Indifferent to the notion of love, he glanced at his pocket watch then continued, "And after that act of love, and the abortion, did you succumb to other acts of love?"

"Certainly not," Grace replied with forceful indignation.

"After the abortion," Murdoch said, "you terminated your affair with the unborn child's father."

"I did."

"For what reason?"

"I feared that I might fall pregnant again."

"Before you married Charles Petrie, did he know of the abortion?"

"He did."

"How did he know?" Murdoch asked.

"I told him," Grace said, "openly and honestly."

"Did you tell him the name of the father?"

"I did."

Murdoch smiled quietly to himself. He glanced at the jurymen, the public gallery and the newspaper reporters, then said, "You were prepared to tell him, but you are not prepared to tell this court?"

"I had every intention of marrying Charles," Grace said. "However, I have no intention of marrying this court."

A roar of laughter swept through the courtroom. Even Sir Wyndham Trahearne's shoulders shook as he chuckled.

With his thunder stolen, Lewis Murdoch

scowled. He approached Grace, then said, "Now that you have revealed your character to this court, would anyone here have you?"

Grace lowered her head. She was tiring, her spirit waning.

"Charles had a right to know," Murdoch said, "therefore, you told him. For once in your life, you did the decent thing. Nevertheless, by withholding the father's name, you are keeping a secret from this court. What other secrets are you hiding, Mrs Petrie?"

While Grace kept her silence, Murdoch bowed towards Sir Wyndham Trahearne and said, "No further questions, Mr Coroner."

\* \* \*

Exhausted, Grace returned to her seat, beside Daniel. Meanwhile, the advocate glanced across the room to Mary, Charles Petrie's mother. Throughout the proceedings, her presence had dominated the public gallery; she sat with her face impassive, with her features rigid regardless of the words spoken.

Called to offer evidence, Mrs Jennet Quinn glided towards the witness chair. There, she caressed her silver-tipped cane, her gloved fingers inscribing small circles in an obsessive, repetitive fashion.

Addressing Mrs Quinn, Lewis Murdoch said, "You tended Grace Petrie after her abortion?"

"I did."

"Please speak up, Mrs Quinn," Sir Wyndham Trahearne interjected, "the jurors can hardly hear you."

"I did," she repeated in the same soft voice.

"You are a mother of three," Murdoch said; "you are in no doubt that Grace Petrie's 'tumour' was an abortion?"

Mrs Quinn adjusted the glove on her left hand. She flexed her fingers in spider-like fashion. Then, in a steady whisper, she said, "I thought you had already established that fact."

"You are a mother of three," Murdoch said, "so how did you feel about Grace Petrie's decision to terminate a life?"

"She had no choice; Dr Collymore advised her."

"Did Grace Petrie always listen to Dr Collymore's advice?"

"Always," Mrs Quinn said.

"Dr Collymore called on Grace Petrie frequently, when she was ill."

"He did."

"And when she wasn't ill?"

Mrs Quinn averted her gaze. She looked to her left, then to her right, then down to her heavy black brogues. "He would call," she said, "on occasion."

"On how many occasions?" Murdoch asked.

"I do not remember," Mrs Quinn said, her gaze still fixed on her brogues.

"You have lost count?"

"I do not remember," she said.

"Please," Lewis Murdoch cajoled, "try to remember."

Mrs Quinn examined the hickory shaft on her silver-tipped cane. She adjusted her wire-framed spectacles. "Several times a week," she said.

A low murmur in court served as a prelude to a bout of restlessness. Chairs scraped the floor, toes tapped inside leather shoes; people coughed politely and adjusted their clothing.

"Would Dr Collymore stay into the evening?" Lewis Murdoch asked.

"Sometimes," Mrs Quinn said.

"And into the night?"

The woman in black looked up to meet the advocate's gaze. She smiled as though recalling a private amusement. "That is not for me to say."

"Grace Petrie was Dr Collymore's mistress, was she not, Mrs Quinn? What is more," Lewis Murdoch continued, "he was the father of her unborn child. Need I remind this court that Dr Collymore is thirty-seven years older than Grace Petrie, and that he is a married man. Sadly, his elderly wife is an inmate in an institution and has been there for a number of years. Nevertheless, he is still a married man. Furthermore, this married man, a man thirty-seven years older than Grace Petrie, tended her as a physician. Moreover, he knew her as a child. What manner of iniquity is this that a man of such senior years should engage in an improper intimacy; nay, let us call it by its apposite name, criminal connection. What manner of iniquity is this that a woman should engage in such a scurrilous criminal connection? What manner of iniquity is this that a woman should prostitute herself before such a man whilst being in full knowledge of the facts? What does this say about Grace Petrie's character? What does this say about the woman that Charles Petrie married? Bert Kemp said that Charles Petrie would not live beyond four months into his marriage. Is it any wonder that Mr Kemp revealed himself as a prophet?"

Lewis Murdoch turned to face the jury. In sombre tones, he said, "It is the duty of this inquest to determine if Charles Petrie committed suicide, if the gentleman met his end through misadventure, or if he was murdered. I believe that you, gentlemen of the jury, already have in mind your answer."

\* \* \*

Daniel, Carys and Mr Robeson accompanied Grace

back to the Grange. There, they entered the drawing room where Grace tugged on a silken sash to summon Florrie Williams.

When the maid appeared, Grace said, "Pull the curtains, cover the windows; I do not want anyone else to stare at me today. Light the oil lamps and the candles. And bring me a decanter of sherry. You had better make that two decanters because I have guests."

"Yes, ma'am," Florrie said.

"Get to it, girl, get to it; look lively," Grace said. "I have put up with enough today; I will not put up with your tardiness."

"Yes, ma'am," Florrie said.

As Florrie pulled the velvet curtains, Grace sat on a satin armchair and placed her head in her hands. She sighed, then apologized to the maid. "I am sorry, Florrie," she said. "Please forgive my brusqueness."

"I understand," Florrie said; "Mr Murdoch's questions were most unfair."

Grace offered Florrie a wan smile, the smile of a tired woman displaying her gratitude. Then she closed her eyes and placed her head against the back of the armchair.

Meanwhile, Mr Robeson assisted Florrie in her task of lighting the oil lamps and candles, the flame provided by a match retrieved from a sideboard drawer. As Mr Robeson and Florrie lit the candles, Daniel reflected on an incident that involved a factory of match girls. Those girls had complained about their employment – their long hours, poor pay and unsavoury working conditions, which led to poor health in regard to their skin, bones and teeth. The chemicals used, in particular the yellow phosphorus, were to blame; everyone knew that, yet the factory owner dismissed the girls' protests. Daniel had been too young then, too inexperienced to intervene. However, he vowed that when the girls complained again, he would offer them free legal advice.

With the candles lit, Florrie departed, in search of the sherry. While the maid rummaged in the cellar, Grace opened her eyes and said, "Would you care to accept your purse now, Mr Morgan, and depart, for surely I am no longer in need of your services?"

"I would not care to depart, ma'am," Daniel said, "and, if I may be so bold, I would strongly suggest that you are still in need of my services."

"For what reason?" Grace complained. "My reputation is ruined."

"It is damaged, true," Daniel conceded, "but far from ruined."

Once again, Grace offered up a wan smile. "You intend to rescue me?"

"With your help," Daniel said, "I believe that we still have a chance."

Florrie returned with a silver tray laden with two crystal decanters and matching glasses.

"Thank you, Florrie," Grace said as the maid set down the tray.

Florrie retreated, to tend to her duties. Meanwhile, Grace poured herself a glass of sherry, which she consumed in one gulp. Then she drank a second glass before succumbing to shame.

"Where are my manners?" she asked. "I should have offered you a glass."

"Not for me," Daniel said.

"Or me," Mr Robeson echoed.

"What about you, Carys?" Grace asked.

"I will drink wine at dinner," Carys said; "I have no call for refreshment now."

"In that case," Grace said, "I will help myself to another glass; just a small one."

As Grace sipped her third glass of sherry in as many minutes, Daniel asked, "Tell me, did the court reveal the truth about your association with Dr Collymore?"

"It did," Grace confessed, her cheeks colouring through a combination of the sherry and shame.

"You engaged in an affair?"

"We did."

"And Dr Collymore was the father of your

unborn child?"

"Yes, he was," Grace said. She reached for the decanter and poured herself a fourth glass of sherry, which she consumed, post-haste. "What must you think of me?" she asked, her cheeks burning red, her left hand placed to her ample bosom.

"At the moment," Daniel said, "my thoughts are with Dr Collymore; this revelation will ruin his career."

"And for that," Grace said, "I am truly sorry."

She sat in silence, her sherry forgotten, her eyes brimming with tears.

"What are your feelings for Dr Collymore now," Daniel asked; "love; affection?"

Grace cradled her glass of sherry. Despite the alcohol, or maybe because of the alcohol, her hands started to shake. In a whisper, she said, "I gave up all chance of love when I married Charles."

"If Dr Collymore had been free to marry," Daniel asked, "would you have married him?"

Grace raised her glass to her lips. In a jerky movement, she consumed the sherry. "I believe that I would," she said.

"Even if free," Daniel said, "such a marriage would have caused scandal."

"But we would have been together," Grace said. "We would have protected each other."

"However," Daniel said, "you tired of your role

as mistress?"

"I could not risk another pregnancy," Grace said, her unsteady fingers reaching for the decanter.

"Drinking will not help your problem," Daniel said, his tone terse.

Grace sat back as though struck. She stared at Daniel, a woman suddenly sober. In that crystalline moment, she blinked then said, "Sherry will not help me, you cannot help me, nothing can help me now."

"You must give Mr Morgan a chance," Carys said. She leaned forward from her position on a second armchair and touched her friend on her left arm.

However, Grace drifted away, on a tide of melancholy thoughts. She closed her eyes and said, "I wish I were dead."

Daniel frowned then said, "Shall I request that Florrie provides you with another decanter so that you can fulfil your wish?"

Grace opened her eyes. She stared at the decanters, at the sherry glasses. Then she shook her head. "No," she said.

"Therefore," Daniel smiled, "there is hope yet."

The sound of yapping announced the arrival of Meg and Mrs Dot, Grace's Skye terriers, who bounded into the drawing room. They ran to their mistress, who stooped to caress the dogs. Then they licked her face with affection and Grace offered a rare smile.

With Meg and Mrs Dot content, lodged at Grace's side, Daniel said, "I will ask you a direct question; I hope for an honest answer: did you murder Charles?"

"I did not."

"Convince me," Daniel said, "that you tell the truth."

Unbidden, tears welled in Grace's large violet-blue eyes. In a faltering voice, she said, "Do you honestly think that I would invite this inquisition upon myself? Do you honestly think that I would expose myself to this shame and ridicule?"

"I do not," Daniel said. "Whatever your life with Charles, it could not have been as painful as this."

Grace lapsed into silence. She caressed her dogs. Meanwhile, a gentle breeze disturbed the candles, made marionettes of their flickering flames. For a moment, Daniel enjoyed the peace and tranquillity; he savoured the silence. Then he asked, "Did Dr Collymore murder Charles?"

"James was very angry when we parted company," Grace confessed. "He wrote me an angry letter. However, his anger cooled; later, he wrote and apologized. He understood my reasons and accepted my decision."

"Furthermore," Mr Robeson said, "we must remember that Dr Collymore had no access to Charles or the Grange."

"Unless we call to mind an accomplice," Daniel said.

"Mrs Quinn?" Mr Robeson asked.

"Someone informed Lewis Murdoch, revealed the intimate details of Grace's life. And I suspect that that someone was Mrs Quinn."

"Why," Carys frowned, "for what reason?"

"If the eyes of the jury are upon Grace," Daniel explained, "then they are not upon Mrs Quinn."

"She has a motive for murder?" Carys asked.

"In the days before he died," Grace said, "Charles suggested that we should dismiss Mrs Quinn, to save money. He reasoned that since our marriage, her position had become redundant."

"Such talk must have placed a strain on your relationship," Daniel said.

"It placed a strain on my relationship with Charles, and with Mrs Quinn," Grace sighed.

"Eventually," Daniel said, "you dismissed her."

"I had no choice," Grace said.

"You were no longer friends?"

Grace rolled her shoulders. Then she adjusted her shawl. "How could any friendship endure such an inquisition?"

"Our friendship will endure," Carys said. Once

again, she reached across and touched her friend on her left arm.

Grace caressed Carys' fingers. Then she gripped them tight. Grace's fingers still trembled, Daniel noted, while the pulse throbbed within her neck. Slowly, but surely, the sherry and the Marsala were strangling the life out of her. Even if Daniel proved her innocent, if she continued along this path it would lead to the cemetery.

"Lewis Murdoch will question you again tomorrow," Daniel said. "You are innocent of murder; therefore, you have nothing to fear."

"Only further damage to my reputation," Grace said.

"Murdoch has no proof of murder. Therefore, he seeks to sway the jury by besmirching your name. Clearly, he does this under Mary Petrie's instruction. With her son gone, she is dead inside, and out of grief, malice or revenge, she yearns to inter you too. However, we will present to the jury the true Grace Petrie and in so doing we will uncover the truth and right many wrongs."

In response to that statement, Grace said, "You set yourself a Herculean task, Mr Morgan."

"What I ask of myself is of no consequence," Daniel said. "However, what I demand of you is that you will play your part."

"I shall try," Grace said, her right hand

reaching for the decanter of sherry. "But to sleep this night I require another glass."

The new day dawned hot and humid. Soon, Daniel reflected, the storm would break and rain down upon their heads.

Within the makeshift courtroom, Grace sat on the witness chair. She looked pale and drawn. She had slept badly, Daniel reckoned. Would her resolve hold, or would she finally collapse?

"Do you still love Dr Collymore?" Lewis Murdoch asked Grace.

"Our relationship is over," Grace said.

"When did your relationship start?"

"After the death of Gustav, my first husband."

"Not when he was alive and you were living apart?"

"Certainly not," Grace scowled.

"Are you sure?" Murdoch asked.

With her right hand, Grace slapped the witness table. She said, "Having damaged my reputation, you now seek to cast aspersions about my mind."

"You have known Dr Collymore since childhood," Murdoch continued, his tone cool, his demeanour unperturbed.

"He was a family friend."

"Did your first stirrings of passion for Dr Collymore begin then," Murdoch asked, "in childhood?"

Grace extended her fingers. Once again, she slapped the table hard. "What you are suggesting is immoral and improper, and, and...," she faltered.

"Mr Coroner," Daniel said, climbing to his feet, "Mr Murdoch's mind might be in the gutter, but surely we do not have to venture there."

Sir Wyndham Trahearne's moustache bristled. With a frown, he glanced at Daniel, at Grace, at Lewis Murdoch then said, "You will be more careful with your tongue, Mr Murdoch."

"Certainly, Mr Coroner," Murdoch said. The advocate straightened his waistcoat. He adjusted his pocket watch. Then he fixed Grace with an intense stare. "In your youth, did you feel love for Dr Collymore?"

"Dr Collymore was a kind man, always ready to listen and offer advice. Such traits lead to affection."

"Yet," Murdoch said, "when you came of age, you married Gustav, your first husband."

"That was my parents' wish," Grace said.

"When Gustav died, his death cast a shadow of suspicion."

"If so," Grace said, "that shadow did not fall upon me. The coroner at Gustav's inquest confirmed that he died of excessive alcohol consumption."

"Did you attend that inquest?"

"I did not."

"Why not?"

"Because I did not want to distress myself."

"You were not called as a witness?" Lewis Murdoch asked.

"I supplied a letter through my advocate of the time," Grace said.

"And that letter was deemed sufficient?"

"It was."

"Hmm," Lewis Murdoch said. He stood with his head canted to the right, with his gaze fixed upon a minuscule crack, which snaked from corner to corner, across the ceiling. Meanwhile, the newspaper reporters sat with their fountain pens poised, eager for the next word. After glancing at the reporters, Murdoch asked, "Is it fair to say that within months of Gustav's death, within weeks even, you commenced your affair with Dr Collymore?"

"During that time we strengthened our friendship," Grace said; "there was no affair."

"When did your affair commence?"

"A considerable time later, when on holiday, in Italy."

"You accompanied Dr Collymore to Italy?"

"Yes," Grace said. "Although Mrs Quinn was in attendance."

"I see," Murdoch smiled. "Yet, in spite of Mrs

Quinn's attendance, consumed with passion you commenced an affair. Are you a woman of great passion, Mrs Petrie?"

"Mr Coroner," Daniel complained; "I feel that I must object."

Sir Wyndham sighed. He shook his head in weary fashion. "Your questions try my patience, Mr Murdoch."

"Please, accept my apologies," Murdoch said. Through his trusty monocle, he glared at Grace. "Did you enlighten Charles about Dr Collymore and your affair?"

"I did."

"How did Charles react?"

"He was calm," Grace said, "and grateful for my candour."

"However," Murdoch said, "your words festered and over time he grew to hate Dr Collymore; is that not so?"

"Upon occasion," Grace said, "Charles was moved to angry outbursts, yes."

"Even though you married Charles," Murdoch said, "your heart still beat for Dr Collymore."

"When I married Charles," Grace said, "I made up my mind that my heart would beat for him."

"Since childhood," Murdoch insisted, "your heart has beat for Dr Collymore. Furthermore, I put it to you bluntly: your heart still beats for him.

Therefore, you poisoned Charles Petrie in the hope that you could return to the doctor and continue your criminal connection."

"Mr Coroner," Grace complained, "I did no such thing."

Placing his hands on the witness table, Lewis Murdoch leaned towards Grace. With his gaze firmly upon her, he asked, "Have you been truthful in all your accounts to this inquest?"

"I have spoken the truth...," Grace hesitated, "on important matters."

"And on other matters," Murdoch asked, "you have lied?"

"I have not lied," Grace insisted. She lowered her gaze and stared at her hands, which now trembled with unbridled emotion. Her bottom lip quivered too as her eyes welled with tears.

"However," Murdoch frowned, "you will concede that you have been economical with the truth?"

Grace placed her head in her hands. She cried, "I did not murder my husband!" Through heavy sobs, and with her shoulders shaking, she insisted, "I did not murder my husband. And that is the truth."

"You did not murder your husband, so you say; you have told the truth, so you say. Yet, I have a letter, a confession, written in your own fair hand.

If I may," Lewis Murdoch said to the coroner, "I shall read this letter, addressed to a former maid. This letter sheds light on Grace Petrie's affair with Dr James Collymore and reveals that indeed she has been economical with the truth. *Dear Laundon, I am quite satisfied with your apology and, as I told you before, that had it not been for your paramour Field, who is not worthy of you, you would never have been rude to me. Nobody regrets more than I do the circumstances that compelled my parting with you for I like you personally, and you suit me in every way. I will do all I can to procure you a good situation and hope you may soon succeed in getting one. I hope you will never allude in any way to anyone of what passed between my good self and Dr Collymore during my marriage to Captain Trelawney. Let it all be buried in the past and if anybody questions you, please refuse to answer any enquiries. With kind remembrances to yourself, yours truly, Grace Petrie. P.S. Burn this.*"

As Grace swooned and threatened to collapse, Daniel stood and addressed Sir Wyndham Trahearne. "Mr Coroner," he said, "I believe that my client is in need of fresh air and a break from this court."

In perfunctory fashion, Sir Wyndham raised his gavel and tapped it upon its block. He offered Grace a doleful look, then said, "This inquest is now in recess. We shall resume in half an hour."

* * *

Thirty minutes later, the principal players resumed their seats in the courtroom. During the recess, Grace had consumed a flask of sherry, Daniel noted, in a vain attempt to steady her nerves.

Within the courtroom, Dr Collymore sat upon the witness chair. A thin layer of stubble lined his chin, which suggested that he hadn't shaved. His eyes too appeared bleary and bloodshot.

"Until this moment," Lewis Murdoch said, "you have enjoyed a distinguished career."

"I have," Dr Collymore agreed.

"You are an acknowledged expert in the field of hydropathy."

"I am."

"You have treated many distinguished and famous people."

"I have."

In priestly fashion, Lewis Murdoch placed his hands together, as though to offer up prayers for his victim. "And now your reputation is in ruins."

"It is," Dr Collymore said, lowering his head.

"Who do you blame?"

Dr Collymore looked up. He stared at Lewis Murdoch. In a steady voice, he said, "I blame myself."

"You do not blame the lady, Grace?"

"She is blameless," Dr Collymore said.

Snorts of derision from the public gallery suggested that many people did not agree with the physician.

"She is many things," Lewis Murdoch smiled; "however, she is not blameless."

Daniel glanced through the window, to the darkening sky. The breeze had freshened and now it tossed the trees. Seagulls swooped and gathered, seeking shelter from the impending storm.

Meanwhile, Lewis Murdoch said to Dr Collymore, "It must have been painful for you, sir, looking on whilst Charles slept with your lover, whilst he spent her money."

"I had come to terms with Grace's decision," Dr Collymore said; "it rested easy upon my mind."

"By come to terms," Murdoch said, "do you mean that you had found a solution to the problem?"

"The problem?" Dr Collymore frowned.

"Of Charles standing between you and Grace; of the obstacle he placed between you and your lover."

"I did not see Charles as a problem," Dr Collymore said, turning away, offering his profile.

"Come now," Lewis Murdoch chuckled, "we are all men of the world; do you honestly expect us to believe that statement. I venture to suggest that the solution was obvious – murder. You had the means – access to antimony, but not the opportunity – you had no access to the Grange. However, a lack of access was no impediment because Grace Petrie resided at the Grange."

"That is outrageous," Dr Collymore said, his face turning puce, his body arching forward.

"What is outrageous, sir," Lewis Murdoch smiled; "my perceptive comment or your improper intimacy with Grace Petrie?"

"Your suggestion of murder is outrageous," Dr Collymore said.

"Sadly, sir," Murdoch shook his head in mock lament, "I think that you doest protest too much. My suggestion makes perfect sense. You prepared the poison then you instructed Grace Petrie on how to administer that poison to Charles."

"Your suggestions are preposterous," Dr Collymore said, although Lewis Murdoch's verbal assault had drained the heat and passion from his words.

"Are they?" Murdoch asked. "Two people in love find their path blocked; consequently, they remove the obstacle."

"We are no longer in love," Dr Collymore said, his head bowed, his features in dark shadow.

"Do you honestly expect us to believe that?"

"It is the truth," Dr Collymore said. "Grace

gave her heart to another man, in marriage. After a period of private torment, I respected her decision. Our relationship, personal and professional, concluded then. There never was, and never will be, the possibility of a reunion."

"That realisation must sadden you," Lewis Murdoch said.

"It does."

"Therefore, a man, Charles Petrie, died for nothing. Surely, that is the fact that must sadden this court."

\* \* \*

With the afternoon rain pitter-pattering on the windowpane, Grace Petrie returned to the witness chair.

"You have not enjoyed good fortune with pregnancies," Lewis Murdoch said.

"I have not," Grace sighed.

"They have troubled your health."

"They have."

"The abortion upset you and, as a result, you terminated your relationship with Dr Collymore."

"Both statements are true," Grace said.

"Equally, at the time of his death, you had no desire to become pregnant again by Charles. One miscarriage is a mountain for any woman to bear;

two miscarriages in four months must have been a great burden to you. To risk another pregnancy and a third miscarriage was unthinkable, because a third miscarriage might have claimed your life along with the baby's life. Therefore, what were you to do? Your husband was recently married and a man of natural, healthy desires. Furthermore, it is not a woman's place to deny her husband his natural, healthy desires. Nevertheless, in desperation, you sought to avoid another pregnancy."

Lewis Murdoch paused. He removed his monocle and paid great attention to its rim. While studying the rim, he said, "I understand that married women perform certain sexual acts even though those acts are regarded as a sin."

Grace blushed. She wriggled uncomfortably upon her chair. In a faltering voice, she said, "I know not of what you speak."

"Come," Lewis Murdoch smiled, his gaze still fixed upon his monocle, "you are a woman of the world. You have buried two husbands and engaged in a criminal connection, an illegal intimacy. You do know of what I speak."

With a petulant look marring her face, Grace turned away from the witness table. "I refuse to answer any more of your questions. They are not relevant to my husband's death."

"But they are, Mrs Petrie."

Lewis Murdoch replaced his monocle. He pushed a top hat to one side and positioned his hands on the witness table. Indeed, the witness table was loaded with so many top hats that it looked like a relic from a milliner's conference.

With his tone as glassy as his stare, Lewis Murdoch turned to Grace and said, "Charles demanded his conjugal rights, didn't he, Mrs Petrie?"

"He did," Grace whispered.

"And when you were in recovery from your first miscarriage, and unable to fulfil your natural role as wife, you offered him an alternative."

"Alternative?" Grace frowned. She turned to face Lewis Murdoch.

"Do I need to expound upon the graphic details, Mrs Petrie?"

Grace scowled. She thumped the witness table with her right fist. Then, with her cheeks turning scarlet, she said, "I did not offer him anything of the sort."

"If that is so," Lewis Murdoch asked, "what happened within your marriage? How did Charles claim satisfaction in the marital bed?"

Grace placed her fingers to her face. She covered her eyes. She closed her eyes. Then she whispered, "He forced me."

"He forced you to perform unnatural

congress?"

Grace lowered her hands. She opened her eyes and stared at the throng, at the multitude of people crammed into the courtroom. "Please," she begged, "save me from this humiliation. I speak to you as gentlemen, as Britons, please, save me."

Daniel stood. He walked over to Grace and placed a hand on her left shoulder. From his waistcoat pocket, he removed a silk handkerchief and eased it into her hand. She mumbled a quiet, "Thank you." Then she placed the handkerchief to her crying eyes.

"Mr Coroner," Daniel said, "I believe that we have indulged Mr Murdoch for long enough."

"With respect, Mr Coroner," Murdoch said, "this line of questioning will lead to the final proof."

Sir Wyndham Trahearne sighed. He stared at his gavel. He stared at the people gathered in the courtroom. He paid close attention to the members of the press. He reflected upon them, upon the fact that they were sitting in judgement on him. With a heavy heart, he said, "Proceed, Mr Murdoch."

Murdoch bowed in gratitude. Then, without any further preamble, he said, "Did you take pleasure in this unnatural congress?"

"Damn you to hell!" Grace yelled.

"I suggest not," Murdoch said. "And I further suggest that your husband's unwelcome demands were the final straw. The night he swallowed poison he proposed that he should sleep in your bed. Yet, exhausted from your first day out after your confinement, you sought to dissuade him. However, he would not be denied. Therefore, you chose that moment to enact the plot, hatched between yourself and Dr Collymore; you chose that moment to poison Charles Petrie with antimony."

Satisfied that he had landed the final blow, Lewis Murdoch returned to his chair where he rewarded himself with a self-righteous smile.

* * *

At the Grange, Florrie drew the heavy velvet curtains to shut out the thunderstorm that had developed during the afternoon. She lit the candles and the oil lamps. Then she supplied Grace with a decanter of sherry.

As Florrie withdrew, Grace gulped her sherry. Meanwhile, Daniel, Carys, Mr Robeson, Meg and Mrs Dot sat around in a circle, their presence warming the drawing room, their eyes upon Grace.

"I am still moved to admire this decanter," Daniel said, caressing the fine glass vessel, which adorned a stout, ebonized cabinet. "You kept the decanter, even when broken, not only for its beauty, but also because it reminded you of Dr Collymore."

"I did," Grace sighed; "it reminded me of our holiday in Italy and the happiest days of my life." She cast her eyes down and stared into her sherry. "Now these are the darkest days." With a tear trickling down her cheek, she tilted her head back, gulped her sherry and replenished her glass. After consuming its contents, she said, "I will not return to the inquest; it is an inquisition!"

"Your absence will condemn you," Daniel said.

"I am already condemned," Grace complained. "The people in the public gallery, and outside the courtroom, laughed at me, they mocked me; I have no life after this."

"Nevertheless," Daniel said, "you must return to the inquest."

"I will not return to the inquest," Grace insisted.

"Would you prefer to offer yourself as a martyr?" Daniel asked. "Because if you do, you will allow the murderer, if murderer there be, to walk free."

Grace closed her eyes. Slurring her words, she said, "I am too tired to talk; I must rest."

Accompanied by Florrie, Meg and Mrs Dot, Grace retired to her bedroom. Meanwhile, Carys asked, "What are we to do?"

"You are to comfort Grace and remain a true friend."

"That I shall do," Carys said. "But what of you?"

"Tonight, I will study Grace's correspondence, to see if it might offer a clue. Tomorrow, I will talk with the coroner." Daniel paused to examine the fractured decanter, the item that meant so much to Grace. He pictured Grace on holiday, smiling, with the sunshine in her hair. Then he eyed Carys and thought, I would love to take you there. With his mind returning to Grace, he asked, "You knew nothing of Grace's relationship with Dr Collymore?"

"I knew of him as a friend," Carys said. "However, Grace kept her secrets hidden or, at least, she tried to."

Daniel inclined his head. He said, "We need to establish how Charles swallowed the poison. Lewis Murdoch has built his case on damaging Grace's reputation; he has offered not one shred of proof. If we can offer proof of the poison and how it entered Charles' body, we can turn the jury."

"How are we to do that?" Carys asked.

Daniel and Mr Robeson exchanged a knowing glance, and a smile of experience. Then Daniel said, "We will find a way."

"You will," Carys said. "I trust you."

"Go to Grace," Daniel said; "save her from the sherry and the Marsala."

Carys hitched up her skirt. She walked with Daniel and Mr Robeson, into the lobby. At the foot of the staircase, she turned and said, "Daniel, I wish to thank you."

"And thank me you shall," Daniel said, "after we have saved your friend, Grace."

* * *

With the lamplight casting long shadows, Daniel settled back in his chair to read Grace's correspondence, which she had forwarded to the court as evidence.

Raucous laughter emanated from the room below as the patrons sampled the delights placed on offer by the Prince of Wales Inn. Setting the merriment to one side, Daniel read the first letter written by Grace to Laundon, one of her maids at the time, on 23rd August 1873 while she had holidayed in Italy.

*Dear Laundon,*

*Please tell Rance that I have no intention of building a greenhouse, and will have nothing ordered from Mould or elsewhere without my order. I only wish for a few bulbs of each sort got for the house, and will leave the quantity in each pot to his judgement.*

*If all is well, I shall be home on 24th or 25th September. Will you kindly get me eight laying hens of the Brahma breed by that time from* Exchange & Mart *– hens that will lay through the autumn and winter.*

*Will you in the course of the next week compare Pegg's prices for coals with Pigott's, as I should like the cellar filled before I return.*

*I am glad all the dogs and horses are well. I often wish that Meg and Mrs Dot were here with me.*

*I am getting on well with the lace for the mantelpiece.*

*With Kindest Regards,*

*Grace*

The letter mentioned Rance, the gardener, Daniel noted, and demonstrated that Grace was indeed mistress of her household, in full command.

The date of the letter suggested that, despite Grace's statements to the contrary, the Italian holiday was not the source of her first pregnancy and therefore she had engaged in further acts of 'improper intimacy' with Dr James Collymore.

With that thought in mind, Daniel read the

second letter, dated 20th January 1876, and written by Grace to her new mother-in-law, Mary Petrie.

*My Dear Mother Petrie,*

*Due to my miscarriage and confinement, I am obliged to be quiet this week or I would have travelled up to see you, but I sincerely hope you are feeling better. Charlie is better, but looks white. I do try, dear mother, to make his life bright, and it did hurt my feelings very much when you told me that I had ruined him. But all is forgiven, and I do hope you will love me someday, as I would do anything for you.*

*With best love,*

*Ever your affectionate child,*

*Grace Petrie*

The letter hinted at the animosity that existed between Mary Petrie and Grace, and Grace's attempt to build bridges. That animosity must have existed from the outset, Daniel reasoned, and it placed Mary Petrie in a bad light – instead of supporting her son in his marriage, she had turned against the union.

On 15th February 1876, Charles wrote to Grace.

*My Darling Wife,*

*Looking back on the ten weeks of our marriage, I feel that many of my words, though kindly meant, were unnecessarily harsh. In future my rebukes, if it is necessary to say anything, will be given with the utmost gentleness.*

*I hold you to be the best of wives. We have had bitter troubles, but I trust that in times to come the sweet peace of our lives will not be disturbed by memories like these.*

*I wish I could sleep away my life until you return.*

*Come back as well as you can to your devoted husband,*

*Charles*

The letter contained words of contrition and affection, Daniel noted, although it also revealed that Charles and Grace's honeymoon period had ceased and that they had started to bicker.

In early March, the couple parted and, on 8th March, in a state of distress, Charles wrote:

*My Dear Grace,*

*My poor mother is glad to have me back with her, and I am sure if you heard the kind way she speaks of you, you would not mind my being with her. Nevertheless, I cannot be happy in the absence of my best of wives. My only object is to make you happy.*

*Charles*

In further letters of that period, Charles wrote:

*My Darling Grace,*

*You make sunshine wherever you go...When you come back I will so take care of you that you will never leave me again...I am always thinking of you and longing for you, and to have your little dogs beside me...My mother has promised to give us the barouche on condition that we put down the cobs. By giving up the cobs and Mrs Quinn, we could save £400 a year, and be as comfortable.*

Daniel sat back. He stretched his back. Then he sipped his wine. Downstairs, the patrons were singing while, in his hands, Daniel held a ballad that bordered on the morose. That tune continued with a letter from Charles' ex-mistress.

*Wednesday, March 22nd, 1876*

*My Dear Charlie,*

*You can keep the money as long as you wish. What made me write, I fancied it troubled you to keep it. I know you give me more interest than I could get elsewhere, but with all I should be sorry to bother you. God knows, every 5s is a consideration to so small an income as mine is. Trusting you and your wife are well.*

*Believe me.*

*Yours ever,*

*Emma*

Next, Daniel read a series of letters dated in April and written by Charles to his mother. These letters contained Charles' final words to his mother and therefore they were shrouded in sadness.

*My Dearest Mamma,*

*Grace thanks you for your letter and sends her best love, and will answer it as soon as she can sit up. She lost Charles the Second on Thursday, a youth of great promise. Trade is dull and I came home early to sit with my better half as Mrs Quinn is in town. I am remarkably well. I am eating like a horse.*

Your loving son,

Charles

My Dear Old Grannie,

Grace is better, but very cross. I went to the library and brought her six volumes of books: three she had read and three contain the uninspired preachings of an idiot. She has finished a pair of slippers for me in a rage, and is slanging me for not being able to tell a good book, but I am not a man of words, as you know. I rode both the cobs the day before yesterday and feel very much as if the muscles in my legs were ossifying. I have difficulty in dragging on my shooting boots, which I am obliged par ordre superieure to wear in addition to a red flannel garment, which is a cross between a kilt, a sporran and a pair of bathing drawers, and has as many strings as a harp. I feel as if I had stays on my stomach.

I am always, dear Grannie, your loving son,

Charles

My Dearest Mamma,

Our financial position is steadily improving. We owe

*about £250 and have in hand £500. As soon as the Chancery dividends, due last January, amounting to some £260, are paid, we will be out of the wood. You may depend upon our not touching our capital.*

*Your loving son,*

*Charles*

*My Dearest Mamma,*

*Grace is still very weak. Dr Marsh orders her to remain in bed, which she refuses to do in this beautiful weather. Instead, she sits outside and stares at the beach. Mrs Quinn is very kind and useful.*

*Our fields are to be bush-harrowed and rolled tomorrow with a view to our getting a good crop of hay from them. I have dismissed two of the gardeners. One could not bother to touch his hat to me while the other would not take a parcel to the station, so I gave them the opportunity of bettering themselves.*

*Your loving son,*

*Charles*

In Charles' final letter to his mother, dated

Easter Sunday, 16th April 1876, he wrote:

*My Dear Old Grannie,*

*I passed the whole of yesterday most pleasantly. I rode Cremorne from nine-thirty to eleven, and on Victor afterwards by the side of Grace while she took an airing in the family coach. After lunch, I put up the lawn tennis net and played several games with Rance. I won, naturally. Altogether, I loafed greatly and enjoyed myself.*

*I am always, dear Grannie,*

*Your loving son,*

*Charles*

The letters contained words of affection, in particular towards Mary Petrie. However, Daniel considered them rather dry, lacking emotion, especially when Charles talked of Grace's miscarriage and the loss of his son.

The correspondence concluded with a letter written after the first inquest by Grace to Mary Petrie.

*My Dear Mother Petrie,*

*A letter received this morning from Charles' solicitor fully confirms my suspicions as to my poor beloved's suicide. Hence his motive for reducing our expenditure as he did not tell me how hard he had been pressed by that dreadful woman, Emma. I wish he had, poor fellow, for I should not have found it hard upon him, but it is a most sad reflection upon his memory that I intend to sift the matter. We have Professor Vernon Pennington's evidence of suicide and shall not allow the living to be under imputation such as is cast upon them by such a wicked open verdict.*

*Yours sincerely,*

*Grace Petrie*

What to make of the letters? Did they clarify or cloud the spoken evidence? Daniel pondered that question as he sipped his wine. Downstairs, all remained quiet. The patrons had taken their fill and now, through the twilight hour, they wound their way home. The letters confirmed that Charles loved money, that he loved his mother, more so than he loved Grace. They also confirmed that Grace felt some resentment towards Charles' ex-mistress, Emma, and that the atmosphere between Grace and Mary Petrie was frosty at best. The letters also shed light on Grace and Charles' personal feelings, feelings that often remained hidden behind closed doors. We are three people, Daniel reflected – the public person, the private person, and the person lost in his own thoughts.

Daniel folded the letters and returned them to the wallet. He would sleep and, in the morning, reflect upon their words afresh.

The following morning, Daniel arrived at the inquest room. There, he found Sir Wyndham Trahearne and Lewis Murdoch preparing for the day's proceedings.

To Sir Wyndham, Daniel said, "My client no longer wishes to submit herself to Mr Murdoch's line of questioning."

Murdoch glanced up from his papers. He offered a lazy shrug. "Therefore," he said, "her absence will condemn her."

"You have offered not one shred of evidence," Daniel said to Murdoch, "not one proof of guilt. Instead, you have sought to ruin Grace's reputation."

"She did that to herself," Murdoch said. "I have merely served as an instrument to expose her misdemeanours to a wider public, to demonstrate why she killed her husband."

Sir Wyndham leaned forward. He cleared his throat then said, "Mr Morgan, could you persuade your client to attend?"

"I could try," Daniel said. "However, I shall require guarantees that the questions will focus on the poisoning, and not on sensation and scandal."

"Sensation and scandal are the stuff of the press," Murdoch said, leafing through the morning newspapers; "look, sir; we are headline news."

"And those headlines feed your purpose," Daniel said. "From this inquest, you will reap great rewards; I daresay the politicians who sponsored these proceedings will offer you a knighthood. However, you do your profession no favours and the cause of justice great harm."

"I have made my points," Lewis Murdoch said, his attention captured by the stocks and shares within the newspaper. "You are free to offer a defence, if you can find one. However, should you wish my candid opinion, sir, I would advise you to instruct your client to confess to the sin of murder and thus save herself from further embarrassment."

"And through her false confession," Daniel said, "you would condemn an innocent woman."

"The woman is immoral," Lewis Murdoch said; "she is guilty. Moreover, you are deluded if you believe otherwise. She married in haste to gain the approval of polite society. Then she discovered that she did not love Charles Petrie because her heart still belonged to Dr Collymore. Wounded through her miscarriages, she could no longer tolerate Charles' romantic overtures; hence, her decision: she chose the only course open to her; she took his life."

Daniel shook his head. He said, "I believe that you have misread Grace and thus failed to understand my client's mind."

"And you understand her mind?"

"I believe that she is innocent," Daniel said.

"Then you are a romantic fool," Lewis Murdoch scoffed.

"I am a romantic," Daniel said, "of that I will confess. However, in the law, I am no fool. I shall prove my case and leave you shamefaced for your scandalous behaviour."

"It is the lady, Grace, who is shamefaced," Lewis Murdoch said, "not I."

Daniel walked to the door. Time was pressing. Within the hour, he would return with Grace for another round of evidence, for another round of public humiliation. However, he offered a parting word.

"Sir," he said to Lewis Murdoch, "your arrogance clouds this room like a fog in winter. However, we shall see the spring; furthermore, we shall get the better of you and walk on into the summer sunshine."

\* \* \*

Daniel arrived at the Grange to find Carys and Mr Robeson waiting for him. They offered each other civil greetings, then they walked to the main door. However, before they could summon the door chimes, Florrie ran out to meet them.

"Sir, sir," she said, "I am most distressed; my mistress is not well."

Daniel entered the Grange. With Carys, Mr Robeson and Florrie in hot pursuit, he ran up the staircase, to Grace's bedroom. There, he found Meg and Mrs Dot, asleep on the bed, and Grace on the floor. Dressed in her nightclothes, she clutched an empty Marsala bottle, while a collection of empty wine and Marsala bottles littered the floor.

Carys placed her left hand to her mouth to conceal her sense of shock. She said, "Grace must have consumed these bottles after I had returned to the Hall."

Daniel nodded. He said, "This is not your fault." Then he turned to Florrie. "We require coffee, by the gallon, a bowl of warm water and a clean cloth."

"Yes, sir," Florrie said. In haste, she turned and ran downstairs.

Meanwhile, Daniel raised Grace's heavy eyelids to reveal red, bloodshot eyes. He noted that she breathed in laboured fashion, while her skin was moist and pale.

With ease, as though lifting up a doll, Mr Robeson gathered Grace into his arms and placed her, upright, on the bed. Then Florrie entered with the coffee and warm water, which Daniel applied to

Grace in turns.

At one point, Grace regained consciousness. She offered Daniel a lopsided grin and said, "I am thirsty. More Marsala."

Daniel shook his head. He said, "My lady, you are a fool."

Grace grinned again. She hiccupped and lost consciousness.

After another round of coffee and warm water, Grace opened her eyes and looked around. "My nightclothes are wet," she said. "This is my bedroom. You should not be in here."

Daniel ignored her. He said, "We have a matter of minutes; within that time you must gather your senses."

"My senses are gathered," Grace burped; "I am content."

"More coffee," Daniel said.

"Yes, sir," Florrie said, and scurried down the stairs.

Fifteen minutes later, after Grace had consumed two-thirds of her coffee, she looked up at Florrie and said, "May I trouble you?"

"In what way, ma'am?"

"To be sick," Grace said. Promptly, she vomited, over her nightdress and bedding.

Florrie glanced at Grace and Daniel. She pulled a face, then said, "Not to worry, sir; I will clean that up."

"Thank you, Florrie," Daniel said.

While Florrie set about her task, Daniel instructed Pegram, Grace's groom, to ride at speed to the Seabank Hotel; there, he would ask Sir Wyndham Trahearne to delay proceedings. With a leading advocate and the chief witness in absentia, Sir Wyndham would have no choice but to acquiesce. However, the delay would not place Grace in the court's good favour.

"I speak with a thick tongue and a sore head," Grace said.

"But at least you speak," Daniel smiled. He turned to Florrie and Carys. "Grace needs to wash and dress; can you assist her?"

"We will," they said.

Daniel and Mr Robeson retired from Grace's bedroom. They walked downstairs and sought the comfort of the drawing room. There, they stared through the large picture window to the flowers refreshed by the rain, to the memory of yesterday's thunderstorm, to the promise of today and a clear blue sky.

"If Grace is innocent," Mr Robeson said, "who served Charles the poison; Florrie?"

"No," Daniel said, "she is loyal; she is innocent."

Upon reflection, Mr Robeson nodded. He said,

"I believe that you speak the truth. However, what of Dr Collymore?"

"Through what means?" Daniel asked. "After the marriage, he had no access to Charles or the Grange."

"Then what of the groom, Bert Kemp?"

Daniel shrugged. He said, "I echo my words regarding Dr Collymore."

"That leaves us with Mrs Quinn," Mr Robeson said.

"She has something of the dark about her," Daniel said, "of that, I confess."

With Carys and Florrie at her side, Grace entered the drawing room. Dressed in her black crêpe mourning dress and heavy jet jewellery, she appeared ready for court.

"Are you feeling better?" Daniel enquired.

"I feel unsteady," Grace said. She placed one hand to her forehead while the other sought an armchair, craving its support.

"Don't worry," Carys said, "we will sustain you in court."

Grace leaned against the armchair. She closed her eyes. "I will remain true to my word," she said; "I will not return to court."

Mr Robeson glanced at Daniel. Then he stepped forward, his powerful presence dominating the room. "Mrs Petrie, if I may speak."

Grace opened her eyes and, with Carys' assistance, she sat on the armchair. "Of course, Mr Robeson; what do you wish to say?"

"I have listened at the inquest to all the witnesses; I have listened to your testimony. I speak as a man when I say that you still hold my respect."

"Thank you, sir," Grace said. She inclined her head and offered a wan smile.

"Furthermore," Mr Robeson said, "I am reminded that I have listened to harsh words all my life, on account of the colour of my skin. At times, those words have hurt me, at other times they have made me stronger in mind and sinew. People look at me, and I know what they are thinking. People walk across the street, rather than walk in my shadow. With each slight, each insult, I feel hurt. However, that hurt then turns into strength. In my youth, I was rebellious, bitter. Now, I am my own man. Through hurt, I have discovered who I am. Cruel glances and vindictive insults no longer wound me because I know who I am. I understand myself; therefore, it does not matter if people do not understand me. It does not matter when they talk in whispers behind my back because when I look into my shaving glass I can address myself with honesty; did I do a fair day's work for a fair day's wage? Yes, I did. Did I remain loyal to my friends? Yes, I did. Did I honour my word? Yes, I did. I know who I am. Through this inquest, you have come to understand who you are. Through your actions and endeavours, you have made mistakes. However, you made those mistakes whilst following your heart. I believe that you have the capacity to be true to yourself. What is more, when you are true to yourself, harsh words, cruel stares and unfriendly gestures no longer matter. All that matters is your will to walk on, and your determination to remain true to yourself. It does not matter what polite society thinks of you, as long as you challenge your own doubts with honesty and integrity. Mr Morgan will save you from the jury; I have seen him perform such miracles in the past. However, to save you, you must grant him the opportunity. Now, will you stand up as the true Grace Petrie and walk proud into that court?"

Unaided, Grace climbed to her feet. She inclined her head towards Mr Robeson and said, "I will."

* * *

Grace walked into court on Mr Robeson's arm. Meanwhile, Daniel paused to study the crowd who, since the first day, had quadrupled in number. Indeed, some of the well-heeled gentlemen were bribing police officers to gain access to the courtroom. However, Daniel did not wait for that outcome, for the crux of the matter lay within.

After issuing his apologies to Sir Wyndham Trahearne and the jurymen, Daniel called Grace to the witness chair. He allowed her a moment, to compose herself, then said, "I know this is unpleasant for you, but could you please cast your mind back to the night Charles was taken ill."

"I shall try," Grace said.

"Before retiring to his room, indeed, before dinner, he felt out of sorts; is that correct?"

"That is correct," Grace said.

"Could you please explain why he felt out of sorts?"

"His horse had bolted," Grace said, "he had a toothache, he had lost money on the stock market and he had received an angry letter from his mother."

Daniel glanced across the courtroom to the immobile, impassive features of Mary Petrie, Charles' mother. Had she poisoned her son's mind, through her letters? Had she moved him to take his own life?

"What did the letter say?" Daniel asked.

"Charles did not show the letter to me," Grace said; "he burned it."

"He did not divulge its contents?"

"He did not."

"Did Charles frequently receive letters from his mother?"

"He did," Grace said.

"And what of their contents?"

"They usually talked of money."

"In what context?"

"Charles owed a sum of money to his mother."

"For what reason?" Daniel asked.

"He required funds to repay his loans."

"Charles was a banker," Daniel said, "a wealthy man; why did he feel the need to acquire loans?"

"To reimburse his stock market expenses," Grace said, "and to offer financial support to his ex-mistress and their child."

"Did Charles gamble, at the roulette wheel, or on the horses?"

"Not to my knowledge," Grace said.

Daniel paused. He glanced at Lewis Murdoch, who sat, head bowed, polishing his monocle. Meanwhile, the jurymen sat forward, listening to Grace's every word.

Daniel smiled at Grace. He said, "I invite you to be candid with me, Mrs Petrie; why did you marry Charles?"

"I found him charming," Grace said, "good company."

"Did you love him?"

"I felt a warm affection for him. I hoped that one day such affection would develop into love."

"Why did he marry you?" Daniel asked.

Grace raised her left shoulder. She offered a diffident shrug. With her right hand, she reached for her shawl and pulled it around her shoulders. Then, while glancing down, she said, "I assumed that Charles married me for love."

"And not for money?" Daniel asked.

"Later," Grace said, "I discovered that he had a mania for money."

"You argued about money?"

"We did."

"How did those arguments start?"

"Usually," Grace said, "with a letter from his mother."

"She meddled in your affairs?"

"She did."

"And when you were not in dispute over money?"

"We lived a civil life; like an ordinary couple."

"Did words of love often pass between you?" Daniel asked.

"Charles was a banker," Grace said; "he knew the language of the ledger; he was often dry with words of love."

"When apart," Daniel asked, "did you write to each other?"

"We did."

"And in those letters did you express your love?"

"I did."

Daniel glanced down to the witness table and his legal papers. From those papers, he extracted a sheaf of letters, bound with a red ribbon.

"I have a selection of your correspondence here," Daniel said. "May I quote from your letters?"

"You may," Grace said, inclining her head.

Daniel unfurled a letter, written on the 10th April to a relative, a cousin, in Grace's small, neat hand. He read, *"Charlie is very well, and equally happy. He has been so good and kind to me while I have been ill. Mrs Quinn is pretty well and has been all kindness to me. I do not know what I should do without her. I eat more than I did, but I am weak. My back is very painful. Your ever loving, Grace."*

Then, from another letter, dated the 20th January, he read, *"Charlie and I are as happy as we possibly can be, and have never had an unkind word yet. I bless the day I married him."*

"And finally," Daniel said, "excerpts from Grace's letters written to Charles. *I miss you, my darling, dreadfully; when you return I will take care of your every whim. I cannot be happy in the absence of my husband; my only object is to make you happy. My dearest Charlie, you are the air that I breathe; I cannot imagine living a day without you."*

Daniel turned to the jury and said, "I suggest, gentlemen, that these are hardly the words of a murderess."

He paused while the jurymen absorbed his words. Some nodded sagely, while others looked on, their expressions thoughtful. Meanwhile, a significant majority glared at Grace, their features grim.

With his gaze upon Grace, Daniel said, "Would it be fair to say that Charles had a dark and a light side to his character?"

"It would."

"Your first husband, Gustav, beat you. Did Charles ever raise his hands to you, in anger?"

"On one occasion," Grace said, "he did."

"And what of his reaction after striking you?"

"He cried."

"Why did he strike you?" Daniel asked.

"We were in disagreement."

"Over money?"

"Yes."

"Please elaborate," Daniel said.

"Charles wanted to put down the horses and dispense with Mrs Quinn's services."

"How did you respond?"

"I told Charles that the horses were an integral part of my life and, at that time, Mrs Quinn was an important member of our household."

"And what of Charles' reaction?"

"He agreed that I could keep two of the horses and that he would offer further reflection upon Mrs Quinn."

"When Charles died," Daniel said, "you knew from experience that there would be an inquest."

"I did."

"You knew because you had endured a similar experience with Gustav."

"I was aware of the procedure," Grace said.

"You must have feared that an inquest would delve into your past and expose scandal."

"I feared that greatly, yes."

"And thanks to Mr Murdoch," Daniel said, "that fear has come to pass."

Daniel offered Grace a reassuring smile. Then he turned to face the jury.

"Gentlemen, I suggest that no woman in Mrs Petrie's position would perform an action, would perform the act of murder, in the full knowledge that it would expose her past. Mr Murdoch has sought to darken my client's character. However, in so doing, he has revealed the very reason why Grace Petrie would not commit murder, no matter how bleak her relationship with Charles, no matter how dark. I say this because the act of murder would lead to an inquest and an inquest would lead to the exposure of her past. Would any woman in this courtroom willingly submit herself to this ordeal? I suggest not. Furthermore, I propose to you, gentlemen of the jury, that you know your women, and if placed in your position they would find sympathy for my client. They would judge that if Charles Petrie consumed poison through malice, that malice did not reside at Grace's hand or within her heart."

Daniel glanced at Sir Wyndham Trahearne and the coroner called an adjournment. In a state of nervous exhaustion and near collapse, Grace could rest, at least for one day.

* * *

With evening drawing in, Daniel and Mr Robeson found themselves in Charles Petrie's bedroom. There, Mr Robeson said, "I believe that you have placed the jury in two minds."

"Now I must place them in one mind," Daniel said, "so that they find in our favour."

Daniel glanced around the bedroom, to the bay window and a smaller side window; to the grate, devoid of any flame; to a gas lamp, a large bed and a chest of drawers. As before, a small clock sat upon the chest of drawers, its tick loud and threatening within the silence.

Daniel was staring at the clock when Florrie entered the bedroom. She inclined her head and said, "You called for me, sir."

"Indeed, Florrie; enter; we must talk."

Florrie walked to the centre of the bedroom. There, she stood, with her elfin features pensive, with her small hands placed upon her apron, smoothing its fine lace.

Daniel smiled at Florrie. He said, "You were the first person to see Charles when he was taken ill."

"That is correct, sir."

"He was preparing for his bath; is that right?"

"Yes, sir."

"He was dressed in his nightshirt?"

"Yes, sir; he had changed into his nightshirt while waiting for me to prepare his bath."

"While you were in the bathroom," Daniel asked, "was Charles in this bedroom?"

"I believe so, sir," Florrie said.

"Did he eat any food or take any drink in this bedroom?"

"No, sir; no food was brought up to him, but he did drink water from his jug."

"Did he use a tumbler?"

"No, sir; he drank straight from the jug."

"Did he often drink straight from the jug?"

"Every night, sir," Florrie said. "I believe I told you this the first day we met."

Daniel smiled. "Indeed you did." Then he asked, "Did you prepare the drinking water?"

"Yes, sir. But as God is my witness, I did not poison the master."

"I am not accusing you," Daniel said.

"Thank you, sir," Florrie sighed.

"Did anyone enter this bedroom while you were in the bathroom?"

"I think not, sir."

"The door was open while you prepared the bath?"

"Yes, sir."

"Therefore, you had sight of this room?"

"Yes, sir."

"Which leaves us with two possibilities; one, someone placed the antimony into the water jug before you brought the jug into this room; two, Charles placed the antimony into the jug himself."

"Why do that?" Mr Robeson asked. "Why invite such agony?"

"I agree," Daniel said, "Charles lacing his water jug with antimony does not make any sense."

With Florrie and Mr Robeson at his heels, Daniel walked into the passageway. There, upon the west wall, the paint had peeled to reveal a drawing of a man's head, and various lines of graffiti, scribbled centuries ago by a hand laden with mischief.

"After his bath," Daniel said, "Charles donned his nightshirt. Then he ran into this corridor and called out, 'Grace! Grace! Hot water! Hot water!'"

"Yes, sir," Florrie said. "That is correct."

"You ran to his aid."

"Yes, sir; that, I did."

"You accompanied him into the bedroom."

"Yes, sir," Florrie said.

"Did you see anything amiss in the bedroom?"

"I did not, sir," Florrie said.

"The fire burned at a steady rate?"

"It did, sir."

"Charles' bed was neat, unruffled?"

"It was, sir."

"Charles ran to the bay window."

"He did."

"To be sick."

"Yes, sir," Florrie said.

"He opened the bay window."

"No, sir," Florrie said.

"No?" Daniel frowned. "Are you sure?"

"The window was already open," Florrie said. "Of that, I am certain."

"Had Charles been sick beforehand?"

"No, sir," Florrie said.

"How do you know?"

"His face and nightshirt were clean when he called me. Later, when he was sick his face and nightshirt were heavily soiled."

Daniel returned to the bedroom. In thoughtful fashion, Florrie and Mr Robeson accompanied his tread. While gazing through the bay window, to the Grange gardens, Daniel asked, "Why did Charles open this window before calling for Grace?"

"I don't know, sir," Florrie said.

"Maybe he felt sick," Mr Robeson suggested, "or in need of fresh air?"

"Both explanations are plausible," Daniel said.

Florrie walked over to the bay window. There, she stared up, into Daniel's thoughtful blue eyes. Sensing that he was on the cusp of a revelation, she asked, "Sir, could there be another explanation?"

Daniel remained silent, as though in a trance. Then he clicked his fingers and said, "Florrie; return to the kitchen; find a small bottle, one that will not require further use, and convey it to Mr Robeson; Mr Robeson will wait here, in this bedroom. I also require a length of cloth. The cloth must be clean, scrupulously clean, if possible unused. In addition, every member of staff should join us. I shall wait in the garden. You shall meet me there."

"Yes, sir," Florrie said. Then she scurried downstairs, into the kitchen.

Meanwhile, Daniel placed his right hand on Mr Robeson's left shoulder. "You know what you must do," he said.

"Indeed," Mr Robeson smiled. "And I will do it well."

\* \* \*

Daniel stood on the Grange lawn, which displayed bare patches, due to the hot August sun. He glanced up to Charles' bedroom window where Mr Robeson stood in wait, then towards the servants' entrance. Florrie ran from that entrance with a square of clean cloth in her left hand and five members of the household staff in tow. The members of the household staff carried oil lamps, to ward off the gathering gloom.

"The gardener, coachman and groom have retired for the evening," Florrie said; "will the remaining staff be sufficient?"

"They will," Daniel said. "And thank you for the cloth." He accepted the cloth from Florrie's outstretched hand then glanced up to the bedroom window, to Mr Robeson. "When you are ready," Daniel yelled.

Mr Robeson inclined his head. He threw a small vinegar bottle, supplied by Florrie, from the bedroom window. The bottle landed on a soft patch of grass and rolled towards a flower-strewn border.

"Very good, Mr Robeson," Daniel said; "now, please, join us."

Daniel waited while Mr Robeson descended the stairs. On the lawn, he led the proud Nevisian, Florrie and members of staff towards the vinegar bottle.

"We fan out at twenty paces," Daniel suggested. "What do you say, Mr Robeson?"

"I say we should find what we are looking for within that circle."

"What are we looking for, sir?" Florrie asked, her elfin features alive with curiosity, her blue eyes bright in the lamp light.

"You will know it," Daniel smiled, "when you find it."

Fanning out from the vinegar bottle, Daniel, Mr Robeson, Florrie and the five members of staff walked across the lawn with their heads bowed. Daniel saw nothing of interest, save for a small deposit, courtesy of Meg or Mrs Dot.

Then, as Florrie approached a prickly green hedge, she called out, "Sir! Sir! Mr Morgan, sir!"

Daniel ran to the hedge. There, from the cook, he accepted an oil lamp and shone its light on the fine branches and spikes. He examined the hedge. Then he turned to Florrie and asked, "When was this hedge last cut?"

"In April, sir, at the beginning of the month."

"When Charles was still alive?"

"Yes, sir."

"And when will the gardener trim the hedge again?"

"At the end of August, sir; he trims this hedge twice a year."

"Then that is our good fortune," Daniel smiled. He turned to the members of staff and said, "Observe; this hedge has grown over the summer months and concealed a bottle of laurel water. A person could not have placed the bottle there, without disturbing the branches, and the uniform growth on each branch states firmly that none has been disturbed. Look closely," Daniel urged; "take in every detail; you will be obliged to swear to this in court." He turned to the maid and asked, "What do you say, Florrie?"

"I say the bottle of laurel water found its way into the hedge in April."

With great care, Daniel removed the bottle of laurel water from the hedge and wrapped it in the square of clean cloth.

"Sir," Florrie asked, her eyes wide in wonder, "does that bottle contain the antimony?"

Daniel glanced at the landau and contemplated a late evening journey to St Hilary. "That," he said, "will be for Professor Pennington to decide."

Inside the makeshift courtroom, Professor Vernon Pennington made his stately way to the foot of the witness table. Dressed in his formal frock coat, and carrying a large leather briefcase, he turned to face the coroner, his lugubrious features burdened with a sense of gravitas.

"I need not remind you, sir," Sir Wyndham Trahearne said, "that you are still under oath."

Solemnly, the professor inclined his head.

Daniel stood. He glanced around the courtroom, at the jurymen, the newspaper reporters and the public gallery. All stared back, with bated breath.

"Late yesterday evening," Daniel said to Professor Pennington, "I presented you with a bottle of laurel water found in the Grange gardens, under Charles Petrie's bedroom window. Household staff from the Grange are here to swear witness to the discovery of this bottle. However, for now, I request that members of the jury and court officials accept my word. I asked you, Professor Pennington, to conduct tests on the contents of this bottle."

"You did," the professor said. Stooping, he removed the bottle of laurel water from his black briefcase and placed it before him on the witness table. "Indeed, I worked throughout the night on your request."

"And your conclusions?" Daniel asked.

Professor Pennington paused. With his gaze steadfast, with his voice strong and firm, he said, "I found traces of antimony within the laurel water."

"A significant amount of antimony?" Daniel asked.

"Enough to kill a man," the professor said. "Indeed, enough to kill a horse."

To a man, everyone in the public gallery gasped. Whispers reached the crowd in the corridor, which in turn spread to the multitude outside. Meanwhile, the newspaper reporters picked up their fountain pens and sat poised to write, sensing a sensation.

"You are not mistaken?" Daniel asked the professor.

In slow, painful, deliberate fashion, Professor Pennington turned and glared at Daniel. "I do not make mistakes," he said.

"Of course," Daniel smiled. "Please, forgive me."

While the people in the courtroom leaned forward and the crowd in the corridor strained to hear every word, Daniel addressed Sir Wyndham Trahearne.

"Mr Coroner, with your permission, I would

like to explain what happened on that perfidious night. Charles Petrie, distressed and agitated, sort relief from his medicine cabinet. However, with the discomfort of a long horse ride, the pain of a toothache, the loss of money on the stock market, and an angry letter from his mother upon his mind, he lost concentration and instead of reaching for a common medicine bottle, he reached for this bottle of laurel water. You will note that this bottle of laurel water is identical to a common medicine bottle. Furthermore, it is not labelled as a poison. However, a scratch on the underside of the bottle would alert the person who placed it there to its true contents. Suitably distracted and burdened by his woes, Charles drank from this bottle of laurel water, believing its contents to be a pain relieving medicine. Discovering his error, and to his horror, he opened the bedroom window and threw the bottle into the hedge. Then the first effects of the poison gripped him and he ran into the corridor, seeking help. Florrie, the maid, rushed to his aid, and you know the rest. However," Daniel said, "I have more to tell. Yesterday evening, I asked Professor Pennington to examine the contents of another bottle."

"That you did, sir," Professor Pennington said.

"With your permission, Mr Coroner, I would like to explain the origins of this bottle and its significance in this case."

Daniel paused while Professor Vernon Pennington removed the second bottle from his black briefcase and placed it upon the witness table.

"This bottle," Daniel said, "a fine decanter was purchased in Italy by Grace Petrie as a memento of her visit. She supplied it with Marsala and placed it at her bedside to sip from as a nightcap. Unfortunately, during a night of restless sleep, she knocked the decanter on to the floor and fractured its glass. However, the decanter was precious to her, along with its associated memories."

Daniel paused. He glanced at Grace who, in turn, gazed at Dr Collymore. The physician looked in better spirits today, smarter in appearance, more like his old self.

"Precious as an object," Daniel continued, "and containing so many memories, Grace placed the decanter on a cabinet as an ornament. She poured the Marsala away. However, she did not wash the bottle for fear that the glass might shatter." Turning to face Professor Pennington, Daniel asked, "Sir, did you find traces of anything untoward in the decanter?"

"I did," the professor said.

"Please tell the court what you found."

In solemn tones, Professor Pennington announced, "I found traces of antimony within a residue of Marsala."

Shouts, the waving of arms and the stamping of feet mingled with gasps from the public gallery. Umbrellas, although not called for because of the clement weather, were thumped against the floorboards.

"Order! Order!" Sir Wyndham Trahearne bellowed while his gavel sought to pierce the din. "I demand order or else I shall clear the court." When the tumult had subsided into a murmur, he said, "Pray continue, Mr Morgan."

"You found traces of antimony," Daniel said to the professor; "a large amount?"

"A small amount," Professor Pennington said.

"An amount small enough to explain Mrs Petrie's recent ill health and, possibly, her miscarriages?"

"Yes," he said, his voice firm, resolute.

"An amount, small in itself, but significant over time in that it would have killed her?"

"Regular ingestion of antimony over time would kill a person, yes," the professor said.

The waving of fans followed more gasps from the public gallery as the ladies sought to clear the air, and their minds, of this revelation.

Turning to the jury, Daniel said, "I feel that further explanations are in order. How did the antimony get into the bottle of laurel water? I suggest that Charles Petrie placed it there. Where did he acquire the antimony? I suggest from the stables, from the bottles left behind by the absent-minded groom, Bert Kemp. Charles hid the solution of antimony in his private medicine cabinet. However, he disguised that solution as laurel water out of fear of discovery. Some spouses place antimony in their partner's alcohol to curtail their drinking habits; this is well known. Furthermore, it is common practice for unscrupulous people to poison others for financial gain. Shortly after his marriage to Grace Petrie, Charles made his solution of antimony. Each night, he placed a drop of that solution in Grace's bedtime drink. Why? Was this the act of a loving husband, someone desperate to curtail his wife's craving for alcohol? Or was it the act of a man intent on murder so that he could inherit his wife's money? Only Charles could truthfully answer that question, but I feel sure that people familiar with this case will form their own opinions. However, we are not here to pass judgement on Charles Petrie, we are here to determine how he consumed antimony. Did Charles Petrie meet his death through suicide, misadventure, or murder? Who poisoned Charles Petrie? With Professor Pennington's evidence placed before us, I believe there is no doubt – Charles Petrie poisoned Charles Petrie."

\* \* \*

While the jurymen retired to consider their verdict, Daniel turned to Mr Robeson and said, "I believe that Mrs Petrie is in need of some fresh air."

With Carys at their side, Daniel, Grace and Mr Robeson strolled along the promenade. Outside, the air was fresh, a reminder that soon the golden glow of August would give way to the golden leaves of autumn. A reminder too that soon Daniel would return to his practice in Cardiff. A coal cutter, sailing towards the horizon, served to underline that fact.

"Thank you," Carys said, her gaze following Daniel's to the horizon.

"It is not done yet," he said. "First, the jury must decide."

"Nevertheless, thank you," Carys said. "Whatever they decide, we could not have asked for a better advocate."

Daniel led his friends, for they had become friends, not mere clients, towards a row of deck chairs. And there they sat with the sun warming their faces, with the sea breeze ruffling their hair. Behind them, on the road, horses and carts trundled along. Meanwhile, the crowd milled around with impatience; some stared at Grace while others sought news from the hotel.

A whisper rippled through the crowd and reached Mr Robeson's ears. In turn, he leaned towards Daniel and said, "The jurymen are returning to the inquest room."

"They have not deliberated long," Daniel said.

"That means they speak with one voice."

"For, or against us?"

"Let us find out," Mr Robeson grinned.

Inside the inquest room, Sir Wyndham Trahearne turned to the foreman of the jury and said, "Have you reached a verdict upon which you are all agreed?"

The foreman, a middle-aged man with large side-whiskers and a pot belly, stood. He inclined his head then said, "We have, Mr Coroner."

"May we receive your verdict?"

"I have written it down," the foreman said.

Sir Wyndham accepted a note from the foreman's podgy fingers. He unfurled the note, a sheet of plain, common paper. Then, with a stern expression and a firm voice, he glanced at Grace and read, "*The jury in this inquest into the death of Charles Pettigrew Petrie concludes that Mr Petrie met his death through misadventure; and that is the verdict of us all.*"

Cheers erupted in the courtroom, followed by the stamping of feet and the hurling of hats. People, strangers, hugged each other. They celebrated because the jury's verdict had restored their faith in humanity; if a woman as noble as Grace Petrie could stoop to poison her husband, where did that place the women, and their husbands, throughout the land? What did that say about society as a whole? They celebrated out of relief, and in praise of justice, because the verdict had reinforced the *status quo*.

At the head of the witness table, Sir Wyndham Trahearne abandoned all pretence, all attempt at restoring order. Instead, he sat back and allowed himself a quiet, satisfied smile.

Meanwhile, at Daniel's side, Grace fainted. Anticipating her reaction, Mr Robeson swooped to save her fall. Ever ready, ever prepared, he produced a small bottle of smelling salts, which he waved under her nose.

As Mr Robeson restored Grace to her senses, Daniel glanced around the courtroom. Bert Kemp, the groom, walked out of the room with his hands in his trouser pockets, with his gaze fixed on the ceiling. Furthermore, a tuneless whistle escaped from his lips, while his expression bordered on the forgetful.

Mrs Jennet Quinn followed Kemp out of the building. She glided past Grace, without a glance. She had talked of a small inheritance, courtesy of a relative in Ireland. No doubt, Daniel thought, she would secure that inheritance, to safeguard her future, to offer financial security to her sons.

Lewis Murdoch shuffled his legal papers. He polished his monocle and checked his pocket watch. He would continue upon his path to great wealth and a knighthood. The establishment were quick to reward men like Murdoch, Daniel reflected. Indeed, they bestowed numerous honours and great wealth upon rascals of all sorts. The establishment offered rewards to egotists and the selfish – what did that say about them?

Mary Petrie walked from the courtroom flanked by her relatives. She looked neither to her left nor her right. Her eyes appeared empty, while her features displayed no feeling, no emotion. She had smothered her son, Charles, with love, and had viewed Grace as a rival. Now, she walked as a shadow, for her spirit had departed this world upon the day Charles had died.

Dr Collymore paused beside the door. He turned to face Grace. Although smart in appearance, he appeared shrunken, a diminished figure. A married man, he had seduced Grace, his patient, a woman thirty-seven years his junior. He had perpetrated a misdemeanour, been responsible for a scandalous sin, all in the name of love.

Dr Collymore removed his top hat and tilted

his head towards Grace. He offered her a sad, wistful smile. Then he walked into the daylight nurturing the hope that he could salvage his reputation as a doctor.

With Grace restored to her senses, Mr Robeson turned and shook Daniel warmly by the hand, while Carys ran across the courtroom to offer Daniel her gratitude and affection.

The newspaper reporters swarmed around Daniel, seeking a quote. However, he replied, "Another time, gentlemen, another time; now, we must take this lady home."

* * *

Inside her fine drawing room, Grace flopped on to a blue satin armchair. Automatically, she reached for a glass and the sherry decanter. "You have saved me from the hangman," she sighed; "how can I ever thank you?"

"You can thank me by saving yourself from yourself," Daniel smiled.

Grace paused with the decanter in her right hand. She gazed at the decanter, at Daniel, at Carys, at Mr Robeson. Then she made up her mind. Placing the decanter on a small mahogany table, she reached for a silken sash and summoned her maid.

"Florrie," Grace said, "kindly remove the

sherry and the Marsala from my presence; kindly remove them from the Grange."

"Yes, ma'am," Florrie said, placing the decanter on a silver tray, offering up a broad smile.

"In regard to the sherry," Daniel said, "today will be easy; however, tomorrow might be hard."

While Grace pondered that point, Carys said, "I know of a physician in Brecon. With your permission, I shall contact him."

"Thank you, Carys," Grace said; "I shall visit him and take his cure."

"And when you return," Carys smiled, "I will be here for you."

Grace closed her eyes, to absorb a moment of peace, of tranquillity. After a period of reflection, she opened her eyes and said, "I have peered into the abyss and decided that I do not wish to enter there; I will not disappoint you; I will not betray your loyalty or your friendship."

Then she smiled as Meg and Mrs Dot bounded into the room.

While Grace caressed her dogs, Daniel said, "I must ask; was Charles trying to poison you, or free you from your addiction?"

Grace stroked her dogs. She played with their ears. Mrs Dot yapped at Meg, and Grace hushed her to silence. Then, in answer to Daniel's question, she said, "At times, Charles had my best interests at heart; at other times, he had a mind only for money. On his deathbed, he talked only of love. Did he speak through affection or a guilty conscience? At this moment, I do not have a mind to judge."

Daniel inclined his head. He said, "And what of the future?"

"I intend to get well, to ride my horses and tend my gardens."

"And if people should speak ill of you or slight your reputation?"

Grace turned and stared at the proud Nevisian. She said, "I shall stand tall and recall Mr Robeson's words."

\* \* \*

Daniel returned to the Prince of Wales Inn where he packed his belongings in preparation for his return to Cardiff.

He was weighing a heavy law book in his left hand when Mr Robeson entered the room.

"I have a message," Mr Robeson said; "a lady wishes to see you, on the sand dunes."

Daniel placed his law book in his travel bag. Then he wandered on to the sand dunes, where he found Carys Beaumond.

In a state of nervous agitation, Carys twirled her parasol in her right hand. "Soon," she said, "you will return to Cardiff."

Daniel inclined his head. He said, "I have my practice to run."

"Will you return to Sker?"

"If someone offers me good reason," Daniel said," I am sure I will."

Carys gripped her parasol tight. She gave the brightly coloured sunshade another vigorous twirl. "What if I offered you good reason?" she asked.

"What do you have in mind?" Daniel smiled.

"A place at the Hall," Carys said.

"A place?" Daniel frowned.

"As my husband." Carys spoke, seemingly, without breath. In a swoon, she placed the tip of her parasol to the ground for fear that she might faint. "Or am I being presumptuous?" she asked.

"I have little money," Daniel said.

"I have great wealth," Carys smiled.

"Some people might regard me as a rascal in search of your wealth."

"Should we care what some people might think?"

"We should not," Daniel said. "However, isn't it the gentleman's place to propose to the lady?"

Carys turned her head away, for fear of rejection. She closed her eyes and held out her left hand. "Do it then," she pleaded, "and end this torture."

Daniel dropped to his left knee. He took hold of, and kissed, Carys' left hand. "Carys Beaumond," he said, "will you be my wife?"

Carys squealed. She dropped her parasol, hugged Daniel and kissed him on the lips. "I will," she sighed, "with all my heart."

The kiss lingered. Then Daniel picked up the parasol and placed it over his left shoulder. He took hold of Carys' left hand and they walked together, towards the large freshwater pool.

"I will still practice law," Daniel said, "after our wedding."

"You must," Carys insisted. "You must continue your good work. You could establish an office here, or commute to Cardiff. Or run two offices..."

"All sound congenial to me," Daniel smiled.

"Of course," Carys said, leaning her head against his right shoulder, "we shall have children."

"I was thinking ten," Daniel said.

"I was thinking two," Carys scowled.

Daniel laughed. He said, "I am sure we will find a compromise."

They walked on, only to pause beside the freshwater pool. As the giant orange ball of the sun kissed the horizon, it transformed the sky into shades of burnt sienna, and the sea and the pool into liquid gold.

While gazing at the pool, Carys said, "Of course, you must share our marriage bed with another companion."

"Another companion?" Daniel frowned.

"My books," Carys smiled.

Daniel sighed then said, "That sounds agreeable to me."

"Then it is settled," Carys said; "we shall be together."

As they walked around the pool, she enthused, "There is so much to prepare. Mr Robeson can be your best man and Grace the maid of honour."

Daniel smiled at the suggestion. He hugged Carys and kissed her again. Then he peered across the sand dunes to the proud walls of the Grange.

"And when you have translated all your pages," Daniel said, "maybe then you will find the time to banish the lies and chronicle the truth of Grace's story."

"That I shall do," Carys said, "with a glad heart."

# AUTHOR'S NOTES

What you have read is, basically, a true story. Under the cloak of poetic licence, I have taken liberties with the names, the timeline and the location. However, the scene at Charles' graveside did occur, the professor did offer the jurymen and court officials a glass of water laced with antimony, and Lewis Murdoch did question Grace Petrie in the manner described. In the court scenes, I sourced much of the material from contemporary newspaper reports of the inquest. And in regard to the outcome? I shall examine that later.

First, the true story. I based Saving Grace on the Balham Poisoning of 1876. I relocated the story to my home county of Glamorgan for three reasons: I am familiar with Glamorgan and its history; I wished to retain a geographical consistency with my other novels, which are largely set in Glamorgan; and I wished to grant the story its own identity by placing it in a fresh location.

I changed the names simply because I wanted to write a fresh story, even though I based my novel on fact. Florence Bravo provided the inspiration for Grace Petrie, Charles Bravo for Charles Petrie, Mary Ann Keeber for Florrie Williams, Mrs Jane Cox for Mrs Jennet Quinn, Dr James Gulley for Dr James Collymore, George Griffiths for Bert Kemp and

George Lewis (later knighted) for Lewis Murdoch. Professor Vernon Pennington stands as a composite character, formed from the various doctors who attended Charles. However, I based him largely on Sir William Gull.

You will notice that I named the maid 'Florrie' after Florence. I did this because in my novel Florrie is instrumental in saving Grace, and the play on names implies that Florence/Grace saved herself. In reality, Florence Bravo did not have an advocate as bold as Daniel Morgan or a friend as loyal as Carys Beaumond. She had no option other than to save herself. Sadly, this she failed to do – she drank herself to death two years after the inquest. This sad event was another reason for the change of names and location – the Florence Bravo story is a tragedy; in *Saving Grace*, I wanted to offer a sense of hope.

Florence Bravo drank herself to death because she could not cope with the scandal. The newspapers of the time reported every nuance, every detail of her private life. For a sensitive Victorian woman, this was too much to bear. In fairness, some of the newspapers found George Lewis' line of questioning distasteful, and many of them published articles expressing that fact. However, far too many gloried in the scandal and sensation. With no regard for the human being at the centre of the story, they exposed Florence with their moralistic double standards. In this regard, Florence Bravo's story stands as a lesson, not just for Victorian times, but also for all time.

And what of the outcome? The jurymen in the Charles Bravo inquest were confused and returned an open verdict, which satisfied no one. Who poisoned Charles Bravo/Charles Petrie? *Saving Grace* represents the fruits of twelve years research and within its pages, I believe that you have read the truth – Charles poisoned Charles. In support of my claim, I offer you the following, an extract from a letter written on 1st December 1923 by Arthur M. Channell, Retired Judge of the High Court and Member of the Judicial Committee, Privy Council.

*Dear Sir,*

*I knew Bravo well, was, under the circumstances I am about to tell you, very well acquainted with all the facts provided at the inquest, and I formed then, and still hold, a clear opinion that there was no crime at all and that Bravo's death was due to a misadventure. I believe that Bravo had bought the antimony for the purpose of putting in his wife's sherry.*

If we accept that statement as true, the next question is, did Charles place the antimony in his wife's sherry to poison her and claim her fortune, or to cure her of her addiction? I have a firm opinion on this matter. However, I invite you to sit on the jury and offer a verdict of your own.

If you have any thoughts on the verdict, or the story in general, please feel free to email me at: hannahhoweauthor@outlook.com

I look forward to your comments, and thank you for reading this book.

# THE SAM SMITH MYSTERY SERIES

The Sam Smith Mystery Series is a character-driven series about private investigator Samantha Smith. The series explores a number of adult themes in a psychological context. These themes include domestic violence, sexual abuse, rape, drug addiction, racism and alcoholism. The books do not contain graphic descriptions of violence. However, they may contain emotional triggers for some people.

The Sam Smith Mystery Series is a detective series centred on emotions, with a touch of humour and romance included to add balance and realism to the various plots. The series has featured in the top twenty book charts in ten countries, including six separate spells as number one on the Amazon private detective chart. Audio book versions are available and translations are in progress.

# THE ANN'S WAR MYSTERY SERIES

The Ann's War Mystery Series is a series of five novellas set in 1944-5. Each story contains approximately 15,000 words and a complete mystery. The stories are: *Betrayal, Invasion, Blackmail, Escape* and *Victory*. Ann's story arc will evolve over the series and reach its conclusion with book five, *Victory*.

The Ann's War Mystery Series has graced the top five of the historical mysteries chart in America, Australia, Britain and Canada. The series has reached #1 in Australia and #1 on the Amazon mystery, history and literature charts. Audio book versions are available and translations are in progress.

# Web Links

For details about Hannah Howe and her books, please visit https://hannah-howe.com

To listen to audio book samples from Hannah's books please visit https://hannah-howe.com/audio-books

To keep up to date with the latest releases, free and special offers, please follow Hannah and Goylake Publishing on Facebook
https://www.facebook.com/HannahHoweWordsmith
https://www.facebook.com/goylakepublishing

Hannah's Amazon page
https://amazon.com/author/hannah-howe

Hannah's iBooks page
https://itunes.apple.com/us/author/hannah-howe

## PRAISE FOR HANNAH HOWE

"Hannah Howe is a very talented writer."

"A gem of a read."

"Sam is an endearing character. Her assessments of some of the people she encounters will make you laugh at her wicked mind. At other times, you'll cry at the pain she's suffered."

"Sam is the kind of non-assuming heroine that I couldn't help but love."

"Sam's Song was a wonderful find and a thoroughly engaging read. The first book in the Sam Smith mystery series, this book starts off as a winner!"

"Sam is an interesting and very believable character."

"Gripping and believable at the same time, very well written."

"Sam is a great heroine who challenges stereotypes."

"Hannah Howe is a fabulous writer."

"I can't wait to read the next in the series!"

"The Big Chill is light reading, but packs powerful messages."

"This series just gets better and better."

"What makes this book stand well above the rest of detective thrillers is the attention to the little details that makes everything so real."

"Sam is a rounded and very real character."

"Howe is an author to watch, able to change the tone from light hearted to more thoughtful, making this an easy and yet very rewarding read. Cracking!"

"Fabulous book by a fabulous author – I highly recommended this series!"

"I loved the easy conversational style the author used throughout. Some of the colourful ways that the main character expressed herself actually made me laugh!"

"Howe writes her characters with depth and makes them very engaging."

"I loved Hannah Howe's writing style — poignant one moment, terrifying the next, funny the next moment. I would be on the edge of my seat praying Sam wouldn't get hurt, and then she'd say a one-liner or think something funny, and I'd chuckle and catch my breath. Love it!"

"Sam's Song is no lightweight suspense book. Howe deals with drugs, spousal abuse, child abuse, and more. While the topics she writes about are heavy, Howe does a fantastic job of giving the reader the brutal truth while showing us there is still good in life and hope for better days to come."

"What's special about Sam's Song? It's well written: accomplished, witty, at times ironical, and economical. A lot of the impact comes from Hannah Howe's ability to achieve effects in a paragraph that many writers spend a page over."

"Sam's Song is more than a standard private detective novel. It has real characters, not stereotypes and it treats those characters with compassion and wit."

"Hannah Howe has a great writing style that is easy and really enjoyable to read."

"In Dr Alan Storey, the author has created a strong male character that is willing to take a step back and support Sam in her career decisions because that's what she needs to grow stronger. I definitely recommend this series."

"I so enjoyed getting to know Sam Smith, a private investigator with an abundance of wit and compassion."

"I started the series and can't stop going from one book to the next..."

"Hannah Howe is a wizard with the way she creates suspense and intrigue."

"If you love empowered women sleuths, you must read the Sam Smith Mystery Series now."

# ABOUT THE AUTHOR

Hannah Howe is the author of the Sam Smith Mystery Series, the Ann's War Mystery Series and various standalone novels. Hannah's books are published by Goylake Publishing and distributed through Gardners Books to over 300 outlets worldwide. Her books are available in print, as eBooks and audio books, and are being translated into numerous languages.

Hannah lives in Glamorgan, Wales with her family. Her interests include reading, music, genealogy, chess and classic black and white movies.